Secrets
at the
Rome
Apartment

BOOKS BY KERRY FISHER

Secrets
at the
Rome
Apartment
Kerry Fisher

bookouture

Published by Bookouture in 2023

An imprint of Storyfire Ltd.
Carmelite House
50 Victoria Embankment
London EC4Y 0DZ

www.bookouture.com

ISBN: 978-1-83790-050-3
eBook ISBN: 978-1-83790-049-7

To all the women who still have an adventure left in them.

PROLOGUE

Sleet coming down like icy porridge. A freezing wind blowing inland from the English Channel. The fan never quite clearing the windscreen. The wipers scraping, too slowly. Two children in the rear, singing, tunelessly, two voices squealing relentlessly, oblivious to the tension rising in the front, ignoring my efforts to divert, to smooth, to pull everything back down to manageable levels.

My arm raised to block an easy passage from front to back. My foot on the brake, flat against the floor.

The headlights of a van travelling too fast. The clatter of bricks and stones bouncing off the bonnet and roof.

A small body in a Dennis the Menace jumper at an unnatural angle. My chest rammed against the steering wheel, my hands covering my head, my fingers wet and warm. A thud and a crack and a dead weight falling on me.

One single scream from the back. The echo of crushed metal, the hiss of the engine and the wait – the agonising wait for a second shriek, a whimper, a thread of hope. Any sound at all, please God.

I should have left long before now.

1

RONNIE

I'd taken a deliberate decision when my husband, Matteo, died to pretend to myself that I didn't remember the anniversary of his death. I'd held steady for the last five years on the grounds that anniversaries of any kind were a petri dish of conflicting and painful feelings. There was no need to make an annual appointment with them when the rest of the year provided ample opportunity for a sudden stab to the heart. But on this May morning, exactly six years since he died, Nadia had guilted me into taking some flowers to put on her father's grave. 'You do it for his mum and dad. I don't understand why you wouldn't do it for your own husband.' She rang off, annoyed, even after I'd agreed and accepted her instructions only to take flowers that were in season, 'not hothoused and flown halfway across the world'.

I took the high moral ground by cutting some blooms directly from my garden. Roses felt all wrong given what I now knew about my marriage, so I chose several branches of pink azaleas and headed off on my Vespa.

The cemetery was so huge that by the time I'd parked up and walked a good kilometre via a few wrong turnings, I was sweating. As I drew closer to his plot, I saw that someone was already there. I knew immediately who it was from the graceful way she was kneeling, legs folded elegantly to the side. No mistaking those angular shoulders that encouraged her T-shirt to hang, gently flowing over her curves rather than clinging the way mine did. I slowed my pace but it was too late. She looked up.

'Gianna,' I said, keeping my voice neutral despite a complicated swirl of anger versus indolence. The battle flaring between outrage – 'How dare she show her face?' – versus a dismissal – 'Be my guest if you want to waste a sunny May day hanging round the headstone of a man who led you a merry dance for years but never thought enough of you to divorce me.'

She nodded a greeting, her eyes full of tears and defiance.

I brandished my azaleas. 'You carry on. I've just come to leave these.'

The words were out of my mouth before my brain caught up, but once it had, I decided that I wouldn't be chased away. And especially not by the woman whose long liaison with Matteo meant that all my memories – everything I thought I had – were tainted.

She stood up and told me she was going soon anyway, before an extended fiddling about with the enormous bunch of roses in an ornate vase. Which felt very much like an 'I loved him a lot more than you did' statement.

So many questions still rattled around my brain. I couldn't fathom why he hadn't left me if he'd been having an affair for over twenty years. Was it conscience, loyalty, cake and eat it, fear of public disapproval? Had he perhaps loved me a fraction more than he loved her?

Before I could stop myself, I said, almost conversationally, 'Why didn't he leave me for you, Gianna?'

Her head jerked up as though I'd said the worst possible swear word in church. She flexed her fingers, which were slender and dotted with diamond-studded rings, her nails painted a delicate coral, well-groomed enough to show me up as a woman for whom a swipe of lipstick was already in the 'pushing the boat out' arena.

We were competing for mastering neutral tone territory. She said, '*La figlia. Nadia. Voleva proteggere la figlia.*'

He wanted to protect our daughter, Nadia.

I nodded. It was a fair answer. But even hearing Gianna speak Nadia's name so easily, as though she was part of her life, as though Gianna and Matteo had taken a responsible decision about what was best for her, made me want to kick over her carefully curated vase and run wildly around the cemetery bellowing about the pointlessness of husbands and the treachery of offspring.

I wasn't sure where to direct my wrath. Gianna was an obvious target, not least because she was right there. Her gaze was sweeping over me, her whole demeanour one of astonishment that Matteo had ever married me, with my foreign ways and disregard for frou-frou scarves and tailored trousers. Matteo was also an excellent contender for my fury. I still couldn't compute how he'd masqueraded for nearly forty years as a passable husband – moody occasionally, funny sometimes, generous often – while pouring enough energy into another relationship for her to stay the course for two decades.

It was ironic that most of my anger resided with Nadia, the person who hadn't actually had an affair. Initially, she'd been contrite after the debacle at the hospice shortly before Matteo died. When it became clear from Gianna's extreme distress that she wasn't just a colleague paying her last respects, Nadia's lack of surprise demonstrated she was already well aware of that fact. 'I'm sorry. I couldn't work out how to tell you. I was fourteen when I first saw Dad with Gianna. I shouldn't even have been out. There was a party that weekend and I thought you wouldn't let me go. What was I supposed to do? Come home and blow up your whole world because I'd seen Dad kissing someone in the back of a car? I didn't want to hurt you.' But as often in life, intention and outcome had proved mismatched.

'Did your father know you knew?' I'd burned with the injustice of Matteo weaselling around Nadia, persuading her that it wasn't in anyone's interests for her to tell me.

Nadia had picked at the ends of her scarf. 'Not in the beginning. I got in a row with him one day and said I wasn't taking advice from someone who was betraying his own wife. He begged me not to tell you. I dithered about it, but it seemed too big to deal with. Eventually, I became kind of okay with covering for him because I was so frightened that you'd get divorced.'

I'd told her I understood, because that was what mothers are supposed to do. Forgive their children, absorb the hurt of their behaviour, dismiss it as naivety, as the misplaced loyalty of youth. Instead, the cordial way Nadia had greeted Gianna at his funeral, rather than furiously shoving her towards the exit, had sparked a rage in me that I'd failed to extinguish.

We'd had a huge argument and, this time, Nadia had done what human beings often do. She'd gathered up her guilt and used it to attack. 'Mum, if you'd have opened your eyes, you'd have seen it yourself. Be honest, you didn't want to know. Otherwise you might have asked yourself why Dad spent all those Saturdays at the office drawing up plans to renovate our apartments or investigating properties to convert, which *never* came to anything.'

I stood back to look at the headstone. There was a certain paradox in the devoted husband/father inscription while Matteo's mistress featured in my peripheral vision.

She cleared her throat. I turned towards her. Gianna nodded towards the exit. '*Me ne vado.*' She swung her handbag onto her shoulder and paused for a moment staring at the grave, as though she was in silent communication with Matteo. Her pain seemed so raw in a way that mine no longer was, not in relation to mourning Matteo anyway.

I still missed him, but even hinting that there might be an upside to widowhood was taboo. With the exception of Marina, my friends met any indication that it was refreshing to be able to please myself without considering Matteo's opinion on what I ate, spent or wore with open-mouthed horror. Oddly, that was true even of the people Matteo hadn't approved of and whom I saw more often now. He'd frequently found my friends too loud and too chatty, when, in fact, he probably meant they didn't immediately stop their conversations to ask him how his day had been.

As Gianna walked away, I tried to look suitably sombre, not too merry widow. I arranged my azaleas, pondering on the relative freedoms of my life now that I didn't have to answer to anyone. I had more of a sense of rebellion at seventy-four than I'd had as a student. I'd done the work of men on the farm when I was growing up. I'd studied hard at school and gone to university. But I still never questioned the expectation that I would cook and keep house here in Rome. I had fitted my job as a translator into the crevices of family life, working late and rising early, accepting that Matteo shouldn't be inconvenienced by having to take up any slack in housekeeping or childcare. No doubt I had my reasons for that, though goodness knows what they could possibly have been. I'd put it down to relief that I'd finally found a husband ten years later than my parents deemed acceptable, one who didn't know about all 'the before'. The net result was that I had scurried around when we had people to dinner so Matteo could pour wine and find himself fascinating. I'd kept any answers to enquiries about my translating work to a minimum in order not to absorb any of the spotlight shining upon him. Now I would have stood in front of the light and made shadow puppets for the fun of it.

Footsteps on the gravel nearby stopped me jumping aboard

the same old merry-go-round of questions without answers. Good manners prevented me from groaning as Gianna reappeared, her hands resting on the headstone in a proprietorial way that made me want to enter into an unseemly tussle. She reached out as if to grasp my arm, but thought better of it. She explained that she had to come back because she'd heard Nadia had moved to England after Matteo's death and that I shouldn't blame my daughter for the 'situazione' with my husband.

Even my English politesse had its limits. My husband's mistress was not going to dictate to me how I interacted with my own daughter. Or anyone, in fact.

'I don't blame Nadia. I blame you. And him,' I said, even though that wasn't entirely true. 'And now, if you'll excuse me, I'd like some time on my own here.'

Gianna nodded, her shiny hair catching the sunlight. 'You never opened your heart to him. He never really knew you and he was lonely in your marriage.'

I'd never slapped anyone in my life, but I was tempted to give it a try. Instead I said, 'Go. Now.'

'Sorry for speaking the truth,' she said in the manner of someone who was wishing she'd actually been a bit harsher, that she'd delivered her view of the world with more spike.

I ignored her, turning my face to the sun until I heard her heels grinding across the gravel. Sitting down on the grass, I picked at the daisies, Gianna's words echoing in my head. I didn't want to be a graveyard cliché, but I could see the appeal of smashing my fists into the marble where Matteo's name was inscribed and demanding answers that I could never get.

Time rolled on, and finally the peace, the birdsong, the gentle comings and goings of other mourners settled me. I lay on my back, looking up at the blue sky, sieving through what Gianna had blurted out. Despite my resentment, I could accept the truth in her parting words. It hadn't been a conscious decision to keep myself so closed off, but Matteo's aloof manner had suited me, had, with the glare of hindsight, probably been one of the reasons I was attracted to him. I wasn't looking for someone to share my every thought. Quite the opposite. I wanted my thoughts to shrivel up in a bunker back in England and leave me in peace. The new set that came later, after I'd arrived in Rome in 1978, I wanted to cordon off, separate from everything that came before. There was no room to have one foot in England and one in Italy. I had deliberately disconnected to stop myself replaying how one bad decision had led to another and then scorched through so many people's lives until they had to create their own firewall to save themselves.

That summer long ago, in my early twenties when I took the first wrong turn, I was filled with the arrogance of youth. I'd assumed that anyone giving me advice didn't know enough about how the world really worked. I didn't have the experience to forecast how it might all end. At seventy-four, I didn't need imagination. I knew exactly how events could shake everyone's world, unrelenting, cruel and unexpected.

However, it still came as a shock when Matteo died to realise that I wasn't the only one with things to hide. Some of the things we keep hidden are just bits of ourselves we choose not to bring into the daylight. We don't lie because we don't have to. No one ever asks us.

Matteo never bothered much with my before. He had no interest in travelling to England. 'Why I'm going there for the rain when I can go to Elba, to Viareggio, to Capri?' That suited me down to the ground, though I would have loved to show him the coves where I'd swum in the clear water, the coastal walks above the turquoise sea, the cobbled streets with the fisherman's cottages. I couldn't do that without my parents hearing I was back and I never again wanted to witness my mother's shame. Or my father's weakness in allowing her to care more about what they said at the fish market, the butcher's and the church than my own devastation.

It was never as clear-cut as that, though. Every year I thought I might visit, and every year I found an excuse, until it became a habit and then the norm. In the end, I left Matteo looking after Nadia and went back alone to Cornwall for my parents' funerals. Then once again to finalise the sale of the farmhouse. It was only when Nadia chose to go to university in London that I grudgingly accompanied Matteo a couple of times to the country of my birth. But just London. Never Cornwall.

And Matteo, who raved about family himself, never pursued it. He was surprisingly uninterested in the people who'd brought me up. He was self-centred enough to believe that until his appearance, nothing else had carried any import, that my life had been beige wallpaper awaiting his dazzling portrait as a focal point. I went along with him. I didn't want to look back. No good would ever come from that. Accepting my lot, being a decent person and not creating waves was my penance for the tsunami of trouble I'd caused.

In the end, going along with things had been my undoing: my desire to take things at face value, to resist investigating too deeply. I'd allowed my husband to lie to me and my daughter to hide the fact he did. In different ways, I'd lost both of them because of it.

2

Polperro, Cornwall, June 1971

I'd felt it many times, this nagging sense that wherever I was, there was somewhere else I should be. And that June day, as I sat on the wall overlooking Polperro Harbour, I was trying to join in, to *fit in* with the group of friends that I'd arranged to meet. We'd grown up together, I'd shared homework with them on the bus home from school, whiled away entire summers in their company. But now, at nearly twenty-three, after doing my university degree – 'You always were a swot!' 'Get you, you boffin' – and twelve months working as a nanny in Paris – 'Oooh-la-la, very swanky!' 'You won't be kissing anyone over there, they'll all stink of garlic' – I'd lost that easy connection. They weren't interested in how hard I'd worked to make friends abroad, the buzz I got when people mistook me for a native French speaker, how I missed the café owner across the street doing a deep bow every morning, '*Bonjour, mademoiselle*', as he set up his tables for the day. Their conversation hadn't moved on: still revolving around variations of whether we were going to have a party on the beach on Saturday night, who was dating/fancying/splitting up and if anyone could borrow a car so we could surf at Polzeath.

No one seemed fed up that they were still living with their parents, with the lads all mumbling a variation of 'I don't want to have to do my own washing'. The girls (whom I'd always credited with a bit more oomph) appeared to rely on marriage as their ticket out of our narrow little lives. That particular afternoon, I'd made some comment about the recent Equal Pay Act, to great gusts of laughter about me burning my bra.

I turned my back on them, feeling both snottily disdainful and hurtfully excluded. To the backdrop of the boys wolf-whistling teenage girls in shorts, I watched the boats bobbing about the water. I gazed at the tourists exclaiming over the higgledy-piggledy cottages lining the narrow streets, stopping to admire the white arum lilies and hanging baskets tumbling with African daisies. Lucky them that they could eat their fill of scones and fudge and disappear home after a week. I imagined them heading back to London or some other metropolis far away from my village near Fowey, where I couldn't even receive a letter from my friends in Paris without the postmistress saying, 'I hope you're not intending to elope off to France with some foreign heart-throb'.

Some days, I felt as though I was suffocating. My mum was full of suggestions about how the greengrocer was looking for a bit of help in the shop. I, on the other hand, dreamed of a life jet-setting about the world, translating for the big boss of a global company or interpreting at international conferences. But judging by the success of my job applications, the world wasn't waiting for Veronica Davey and her many memorised quotations from *Le Petit Prince*.

As I sat there trying to block out the juvenile jokes behind me, I noticed a man pushing a baby in a stripey pushchair. He was also instructing a dark-haired girl, about four years old, to stay close to him, to keep away from the harbour edge. She wasn't listening, focused on waving her shiny plastic windmill and blowing on it to make it spin. I looked about for his wife, but he appeared to be on his own. With his Polaroid sunglasses, posh watch and Levi's, he had a suave air about him, a confidence that suggested that out of holiday attire he was totally at home in a suit.

He bent down to pick up the sunhat the baby had tossed on the ground, just as the little girl wandered very close to the harbour edge, pirouetting about with her windmill.

I leapt to my feet. 'Hey! Careful! That's a big drop down there.'

She stared straight up at me, her chin jutting out. 'It's not that far. I can nearly do doggy-paddle anyway.'

Her dad raced over. 'Heather! I said to hold onto the pushchair.' He turned to me. 'Thank you. I need eyes in the back of my head with this little tinker. Only one of me and two of them isn't the perfect combination.'

I smiled, inhaling the knowledge that he was alone like the first scent of hyacinths after a long winter. 'No problem at all. Wouldn't be the first time a holidaymaker has fallen in the sea, but it's usually when the pubs close.'

'You're local then?'

Something about him made me want to be mysterious, enigmatic, sophisticated. Much more than the daughter of a dairy farmer, hanging about with a bunch of mates whose weekend plan amounted to winning enough on the fruit machines to buy a packet of Benson & Hedges. 'I live near Fowey, but I'm actually just back from a year in Paris.'

His face lit up. 'You speak French?'

'*Bien sûr. Couramment. Vous?*'

He nodded, sticking his bottom lip out, impressed, as though he wasn't expecting that. '*Un peu.*' He carried on. 'I work in imports and exports, wine mostly, but also cognac, cheese sometimes. I live in London, but I've got a place in Fowey, so I'm not a total tourist.'

I wanted to fall at his feet, beg him to find me a job. But right at that moment, my friends decided to make a dash for the bus to Looe and Billy grabbed at my arm. 'Ron, we're leaving, come on!'

Before I could say anything else, the man said, 'Mustn't miss that bus! Thanks again for stepping in with Heather here.'

My friends swept me along, and I followed irritably, unable to muster any enthusiasm for the big news that Billy's brother was going to let him drive his Capri when he finally passed his test. Billy topped off his boast with the bonus information that it had an airhorn that played '*La Cucaracha*'. The art galleries of Paris seemed a million miles away.

Three days later, I'd sulked off to the beach at Fowey, fresh from a quarrel with my mother, who had told me in no uncertain terms that: 'You might think you're far too fancy to help Dad with the cows or to go and do a bit of typing at the doctor's surgery, but money doesn't grow on trees.' I'd looked at her, this woman who darned my dad's socks, ran up a new skirt on her Singer sewing machine every Christmas, salvaged every last bit of maggoty apple from our orchard, and felt a profound dread settle on me. I'd grabbed my swimming things, hopped on my bike and ridden at speed to the beach. Forcing the pedals round, I'd strained up the hills until my muscles screamed in order to feel alive.

I flung myself into the cold water, steaming through the waves, a powerful front crawl that left me breathless. Yards out, I bobbed about, trying to still the fear that my future would be parochial and ordinary and that one day I might fool myself into thinking I was happy with that.

I scanned the beach, squinting at the holidaymakers with their windbreaks, deckchairs and cool boxes. I swam back, calmer now, the water working its magic, cooling my thoughts and steadying my emotions.

As I walked out of the sea, a little voice said, 'Hello! I saw you the other day. Do you like my armbands? I can't swim properly yet. Daddy says he can't leave Lyndsey, that's my sister, so he can't come in to teach me.'

My heart leapt as I realised it was the girl I'd met in Polperro earlier that week. Maybe I'd get another chance to speak to her father about jobs in imports and exports. I'd leave no stone unturned to magic up an exit from my dreary life.

I looked around and spotted Heather's dad, who was in a deckchair by the rocks. He waved his newspaper at me. '*Bonjour, mademoiselle. Comment allez-vous?*'

We walked over to him and, far louder than necessary, I replied in French, feeling cosmopolitan and glamorous, as though everyone on the beach would be impressed by my command of the language.

Heather pulled at my wrist. 'Will you take me swimming?'

'If your dad doesn't mind?'

He stood up and held out his hand to me. 'Eddie.' He patted the little girl on the head. 'Heather, you've already met.' He jabbed his thumb towards the baby sleeping under a parasol in the pushchair. 'That's Lyndsey.'

I introduced myself and Heather hopped about impatiently. 'Come on.'

I looked at Eddie and he shrugged. 'If it's all right with you?'

And somehow, that became the pattern of the next week. We left every day, saying, 'See you around.' Every morning I cycled to the beach, my heart barely daring to hope that I'd see the little trio, tucked in their usual spot against the rocks, Eddie with his newspaper, Heather poking about with her spade at the edge of the water.

Finally, Eddie said, 'So we're off to London the day after tomorrow, but we're back at the end of July. I'm looking for a housekeeper to give the place a good clean and get in some provisions. We'll be here for at least a fortnight then, maybe longer.' He peered at me over his sunglasses. 'Do you know anyone who might be interested? It could be live-in. There's plenty of room. It would have to be someone who doesn't mind working for a soon-to-be divorced dad? Well, in about five years' time anyway if my wife doesn't agree.' He laughed, his face crinkling with merriment.

I'd never met anyone divorced before. He hadn't mentioned his wife until now and although I'd wondered about her, I hadn't dared ask for fear of sounding nosey and provincial, as though a dad looking after children on his own was unheard of round our way. I was flabbergasted at the way he referred to his divorce so casually, as though that was a run-of-the-mill occurrence in London. He seemed as glamorous to me as Elizabeth Taylor and Eddie Fisher.

He named a weekly wage that would make me the envy of all my friends and put an end to my mother's nagging about brushing up on my secretarial skills. I wouldn't tell her about the divorced bit. A monumental row already lay ahead.

Excitement rippled through me as though being in his house would automatically confer sophistication upon me. 'I could do that for you.'

He smiled as though he'd known that all along. I didn't care. It wasn't the dizzying heights of an international interpreting job, but it was a springboard away from the farm and a step closer to the life I knew I could have.

3

Present Day

Marina and I set aside two evenings, a bottle of Martini, a bottle of Campari, some Prosecco, prosciutto and pecorino to find new tenants for the apartment Beth had vacated last week. Our mood was celebratory: the first experiment of inviting a middle-aged woman to Rome in order to rediscover her zest for life had been a success. I hoped it wasn't beginner's luck. It had been such a delight to see Beth transform from a woman at everyone's beck and call to a feisty being who did a fair bit of ass kicking herself. Fingers crossed that our next candidate would also benefit from time here to figure out how to wring every drop of joy from the next few decades.

Marina tapped her walking stick on the floor. 'Not tempted to offer the other apartment you've renovated to Nadia and the vile husband for the summer?'

'You think I should? Isn't one new person in the palazzo enough for now?'

I didn't even know why I asked the question because I wasn't going to invite my daughter to live next door, whatever Marina thought. It was probably just one of those silly friendship tests – ludicrous after forty-five years – to see if she would dance the dance of agreeing with me even if she thought I was wrong.

'For what it's worth, yes. You're doing what you always do. Avoiding the issue instead of dealing with it.' Marina had never so much as tapped a toe, let alone danced, to anyone else's tune.

'You wouldn't be saying that if Nadia and Grant came to live next door and started monitoring your wine consumption or shuffling you off to bed at ten o'clock.'

Marina grunted in a way that indicated they'd have their work cut out to control any aspect of her behaviour.

I turned back to the job at hand. 'Let's see where we get to with these. We can't be splashed all over a national magazine, receive a ton of applications, then not deliver on our promise.' I split a huge pile of letters in half. 'Here, you start with these. And don't pull that face. You had the bright idea of contacting that journalist chap to do a story on our – and I quote – "retreat for the broken, the bereaved, the betrayed". You've only got yourself to blame if a gaggle of disillusioned women are leaping at the chance to reinvent themselves.'

Marina sagged dramatically. 'Why don't we do a lucky dip? I'm not sure I can be bothered to read all these women's sob stories. How do I know whether losing your job is worse than being ditched by your husband? If your dog dying is worse than your cat? It's all a matter of perspective.'

I stroked my miniature Schnauzer and said, 'Strega, close your ears. Marina doesn't know whether a cat dying is worse than a dog. Has she learnt nothing?'

Marina finished off her first negroni sbagliato without picking up a single letter and made herself another one. 'There are way too many to sift through.'

I flicked through the stack of envelopes. 'I didn't want to be in the stupid magazine anyway. What did you expect? Instead of the seven letters from the original advert in *The Lady*, we've got about a hundred. And I'm sorry, but now they've taken the trouble to write to us, I feel honour-bound to read every one.'

'I only suggested the feature so we'd get some decent photos.' She nodded to the framed one of us on my sideboard. 'He definitely took my best side. Anyway, because you agreed to do it, I kept my part of the bargain and got Federico's son to carry out the renovations.' She winked. 'Without my "charms", you could have been waiting for another two years to find a decent plumber.'

Far be it from me to burst Marina's bubble, but I wasn't sure that it was a desire to help his dad woo Marina that motivated Federico's son, Renzo. I was more under the impression that he'd taken one look at my crumbly old palazzo containing five apartments and reserved himself a Porsche on the back of future earnings.

Marina sighed and pulled a few letters onto her lap. 'I'm going to choose by handwriting.'

The woman was exasperating. 'I'm going to choose by how quickly they can get out here,' I said. 'The beginning of June would be ideal, so if Nadia asks, I can say with my hand on my heart that the apartment Beth was staying in is taken. And if you speak to her, don't you dare let on that I've renovated one of the other two and that it's standing empty.'

Marina did a dramatic gesture of zipping her lips, which was laughable as her idea of keeping a secret was telling ten people instead of broadcasting it to her whole network.

I unfolded a letter. 'So, this woman has been in the same job for thirty-three years, the department has closed and, at fifty-eight, she's struggling to find work.'

A sneer crossed Marina's face as though only women who

weren't clever enough to find a husband worked for thirty-three years. 'What did she do?'

'She worked for a charity campaigning to reduce how much meat and dairy people eat.'

By way of an answer, Marina tipped her head back, dangled a piece of ham into her mouth and savoured it with a theatrical flourish. I dropped that one into the bin.

I picked up another. 'This woman has got divorced for the third time, is fed up with Englishmen and wants to try a different nationality.'

'How old is she?'

'Sixty-eight.'

Marina shook her head. 'No. Definitely not. She'll be fishing in the same pool as me. I can do without the competition. We did well to find someone for Beth.'

'Technically, Beth found her own man. And are you really going to be chasing men in their sixties? You are eighty next birthday.'

Marina put her hands up to her cheeks and pulled her skin back slightly, giving herself a facelift. 'I know. I know. But I don't look a day over seventy. Anyway, I've had enough of man dramas. I've worn myself out acting as a matchmaker for Beth. I'm glad she finally got together with Rico, but it was a bit dung beetle pushing a great *caca* uphill. I mean, how long did it take her to realise that stupid husband of hers was *un bastardo*?' As Marina often did when she felt very passionate, she switched into Italian for a rant about the shortcomings of men, eventually exhausting herself. 'And as I understood it, Beth is intending to come back again if she and Rico can survive these three months of separation. There's a limit to how many happy ever afters I can stomach.'

I took a swig of my negroni sbagliato, hoping the alcohol would push away the nagging guilt that I should be trying to fix my relationship with Nadia. I read through some more applications. Marina kept objecting to women that quite appealed to me. 'She sounds so dull. We want someone with a bit of spirit.' 'Absolutely not. I can quite see why she doesn't get on with her family. She's not coming here to be difficult.'

I laughed out loud. 'Don't tell me, there's only room for one difficult person and you've already taken that role?'

'I'm not difficult,' Marina said, with a grin but also an air of indignation that suggested she actually *believed* that she was sweetness and light.

I fished into the various envelopes and pulled out a thick padded one. I flapped it about. 'There's more than a letter in here. I hope it isn't some weird hate mail and they've posted us a turd.'

Marina wrinkled her nose. 'What normal person would imagine that? The sun has fried your brain. They've probably sent us the magazine where they saw the article.'

I squidged the parcel. 'No, it's a packet of something.'

I levered my knife under the flap so that I could reuse the envelope at a later date, never quite shedding my mother's frugal habits.

Out dropped a pack of liquorice wagon wheels. I fell on them. 'Oh my word! I *love* these. Used to eat them all the time at university instead of breakfast. I adore this woman already.'

'How did I ever become friends with you? Who gets up and instead of coffee and *una brioche* decides to give themselves black teeth first thing in the morning?'

'It's in my Cornish DNA. My dad loved liquorice too. Always had a bag in his tractor.' I forced myself not to dwell on how much time I'd missed with him, a loss that I'd only appreciated in my later years.

I pulled out her letter and glanced at the name at the bottom. Annie Gordon.

'Let's have a look at her.'

Dear Ronnie and Marina,

I came across your story in a magazine in the dentist's surgery and it couldn't have come at a better time. One, I just loved the whole idea of two strong women sharing their (maybe) unorthodox wisdom with the world. I was particularly taken with Marina's view that youth is a time for fitting in with everyone else but middle age is the time to stand up and say, 'This is who I am, stay for the whole show or leave the auditorium.' Fantastic quote! I've struggled with this my whole life. I've longed to fit in but, at the same time, seem to have too many opinions/too much spirit to be able to conform. I'd love to say I don't care what people think of me, but I do. I'd absolutely relish the opportunity to do something different and take some time away from the people who are angry with me for not accepting their view of the world.

Marina raised an eyebrow. 'She sounds a possibility.'

I could have guaranteed anyone who flattered Marina would automatically catapult herself to the top of the list.

'How old is she?' Marina asked.

I scanned the letter. 'Fifty-six. Taken a sabbatical from her post recruiting new teachers for English language schools abroad. Debating about never going back. Done and dusted with London.'

Marina nodded in approval. 'Enough life to be interesting and enough imagination to believe she doesn't have to live the same way forever.' Her head jerked up. 'Has she got children? I can't stand months of hearing about how marvellous her offspring are. After the age of sixteen, no one needs applause for getting out of bed, running a house and holding down a job.'

It had taken me a long time to recognise that so many of Marina's statements were her instinctive barrier against all the pitying comments about her not having any children. *'Why can't they accept that I'm just not maternal? Give me a dog any day.'*

'She's got two adult sons, but they don't live at home any more.'

Marina harrumphed. 'Has she got grandchildren? I certainly can't cope with stories about seven-year-olds whose violin playing has to be heard to be believed.'

It was no wonder that Marina's friendship circle had dwindled drastically, even allowing for the ones who had died.

'No grandchildren as far as I can tell,' I said.

'What else does she say?'

I read out a bit more.

Plus my mother has died recently, which has caused some 'interesting' family dynamics. I never really understood her and vice versa, and now I've missed my moment. My sister (whom I love dearly) is furious with me for disagreeing with her rose-tinted version of our upbringing. We've had a huge falling out. I hope that time apart will give us both a chance to cool down and find a way back to each other.

Anyway, if my letter hasn't put you off, I hope you will consider me. I can one hundred per cent promise that I will make the most of any challenges you fire in my direction. If I'm lucky enough to be chosen, I can fly out as soon as you say the word.

Finally, enjoy the liquorice, Ronnie – I saw in the article that you missed it and it was easier to send that than British sea air on a blustery autumn day!

Marina puffed out. 'So nothing as ordinary as fighting over a will and who receives the favourite teapot?'

'No, it doesn't appear to be about money. Perhaps that's not what motivates her.'

'*Bene*. Maybe she's the one. There's nothing like a death to give family politics a good stir. If you won't rescue your relationship with your daughter, you can put yourself to good use and fix the sisters. There would be a certain satisfaction in two old ladies sorting someone else's family. Usually it's the other way round. Might be entertaining at least.'

Sometimes I wondered how I'd tolerated Marina for so long. My falling out with Nadia was rooted in specific circumstances. Marina fell out with people because they forgot her birthday, didn't notice she had a new blouse or didn't offer her their umbrella when it was drizzling. Frankly, if I hadn't been a peacemaker over the last four decades, we could have stopped speaking twice a week. But despite her outrageous comments, her jokes that were too close to the truth, her total refusal to sugar-coat anything, she was the closest person I had to family. Behind all the bluster, she was, and had always been, there for me. Tricky, outspoken, infuriating, but always ready to catch me when many others stood with their hands in their pockets. If nothing else, life would be immeasurably boring without her.

Annie Gordon, pack your bags. Let's see if you can build bridges *and* stick to your lines in the sand.

4

The gulf between what I guessed people would look like and the reality never ceased to amaze me. I'd expected to usher in a serious woman with a neat haircut and a navy blazer, shattered by grief and a family falling out. A woman who would allow Marina to be top dog and accept her unsolicited advice without snarling back. Instead, from the car bounced a bundle of energy, long curly brown hair framing an angular face. Black leather bomber jacket, red ruffled blouse and the sort of zippy black jeans I associated with Johnny Rotten circa 1977.

It was time to reconfigure my assumptions. Our experiment of offering a sanctuary and a kick-start to someone who'd hit a rough patch was based on a premise that they'd be so broken that Marina and I would be able to bend them to our will and shape them as we saw fit. But Annie Gordon radiated a confidence that seemed to contradict her claim that she really cared what people thought of her.

'Helloooo! Wow! This is amazing... what a fabulous place. I can't believe I'm here!' The jury was out on whether her loud enthusiasm fell into the 'vexatious to the soul' or 'the big tick in appreciating what an opportunity this was' category.

She hauled a battered suitcase out of the boot of the taxi, waving away the offer of help from the bemused driver. She then leaned into the car and re-emerged with a rucksack and a carrier bag with a broken handle, trailing a sunhat and a swimming costume.

Flinging everything onto the ground as the cab disappeared, she peeled off her jacket and dumped it on her luggage. She strode over and extended a hand. 'I'm Annie.'

'Ronnie. Welcome to Villa Alba,' I said, searching for traces of the vulnerability I'd connected with in her letter. I had the uncharitable thought that she didn't look anywhere near as grief-stricken as I'd anticipated. I told myself off for falling into the trap of assuming that I had the monopoly on how to react to traumatic life events, as though one size fits all.

She pushed her hair away from her face. 'Thank you. It's boiling here already. Is it always this hot in early June?' That whirl of energy dropped like an unpredictable sea breeze and she stood back, her face serious, her eyes narrowing as though she was scrutinising me and forming an opinion. Despite her chaotic arrival, there was a canniness about her and a dynamism that would either prove advantageous or irritating. I understood immediately what she'd tried to express in her initial approach to us. You could love or hate Annie Gordon, but she would be difficult to ignore.

'You'll adjust to the heat, but I strongly recommend getting an early start for sightseeing. Here, let me show you where you'll be staying. I assume you're all right with dogs,' I said as Strega roused herself from a shady corner of the courtyard to wag her tail and sniff around our newcomer.

'Oh yes, I love dogs,' Annie said, kneeling down and fussing Strega's ears until her mouth hung open in a doggy smile.

One big tick in the approval box. Anyone who thought my dog was just a dog was in for a shock when they understood the hierarchy at Villa Alba.

I went to pick up her rucksack and bags. 'I can manage,' she said, but I couldn't decipher from her tone whether it was out of concern for me or an unwillingness to accept help.

I ignored her, saying, 'I grew up on a farm,' as though that explained everything. Whatever her reasoning, she wasn't writing me off as a little old lady. I couldn't stand the way people assumed that simply because you were in your seventies, your arm would snap if you carried anything. Even though it was a long time since I'd looked out over those Cornish fields where I ran free as a child, my farming heritage had not faded: I remained certain I could still haul out a calf in the unlikely event that a pregnant cow should find itself in difficulty outside the Vatican.

I marched up the steps, through the front door and past what I now thought of as Beth's place. At the last minute, I'd decided to test out Renzo's recent renovations by putting them through daily rather than occasional use. I showed Annie up a flight of stairs and into the apartment I'd always liked the best. I loved the bed built into an alcove at the bottom of a tower. 'We've just redone the kitchen and bathroom in here.'

She put her case down. 'This is absolutely beautiful, thank you.' She paused. 'Why are you doing this for complete strangers, though? What's in it for you?'

She had a directness about her, reminiscent of Marina, that I found rather appealing. Far more Italian in style than British. She even reminded me of myself when I was young, bowling into everywhere, sharing my feelings without fear or restraint. A woman without a side, without any thought for a protective carapace.

I was tempted to tell the truth. That alongside the official 'motive' that we'd flagged up in the feature she'd responded to, I wanted to bed-block – or, rather, apartment-block – so that my own daughter couldn't move in. But there was another complex reason. The thing I couldn't even admit to Marina because she didn't know the half of it: I wanted to atone for my mistakes.

But I'd trained myself over the last forty-five years in the skill of making people believe they were on an intimate footing with me without revealing anything much at all. So I said, 'Rome has been my home for over four decades. I came here when I was thirty and lacking direction.' I did an inner eyeroll at that spectacular understatement. 'I'm widowed, I have all this space, and it seemed a shame not to share it with women who need to recalibrate and assess what they want from their futures.' I closed the conversation down by talking her through the various quirks of the bathroom and the gas hob in the kitchen. 'You must keep the shutters closed during the day, otherwise you'll boil.'

When I'd first come to Italy, I'd horrified Matteo by refusing to live in twilight during the summer. I'd thrown open the curtains, blinds and shutters to allow the sunlight to flood every nook and cranny. Eventually, I'd had to succumb to the wisdom of shutting everything against the forty degrees of heat to give me an outside chance of sleeping in this old palazzo where we relied on fans for air conditioning.

As I left, Annie asked, 'Where are you from originally?'

'Cornwall.' I was never more specific than that.

'That's a nice area of the country. Whereabouts in Cornwall?'

She looked at me expectantly, waiting for my answer. But the glorious thing about being older was that it was easy not to reply. More often than not, people didn't bother to repeat the question if you brazenly ignored them. They simply decided that you were a bit deaf, cantankerously rude or not quite right in the head. But never that you didn't answer because Cornwall was where it all began. Where it all ended. Where I could no longer stay.

5

Annie's arrival unsettled me. In the two days she'd been here, I'd attempted to discuss her mother's death to get an idea of which challenges might help her. However, every time I tried to gain an insight into how she was feeling and what specifically caused the fallout with her sister, she made it sound as though mothers were two a penny and not speaking to her sister was no big deal either. Whenever I broached the subject, she shrugged. 'I didn't really get on with my mother. She lived in cloud cuckoo land and my sister was her favourite because she indulged her.'

Even at my age, when seventy-four years had taught me a lot about imperfect maternal love, I fell into the trap of defaulting to a platitude rather than acknowledging her hurt. 'I'm sure she loved you both the same.' Sometimes I was grateful to have had only one child, to not have been put to the test.

'No, I don't think she did.'

I admired this woman's frankness. She'd keep us on our toes.

I felt my way on to unfamiliar territory, confronting rather than shying away from other people's pain. 'What makes you say that?'

'After my father died, my mother rewrote history. Well, not so much rewrote as reinvented. I just couldn't sit there and listen to her delusions. So, naturally, she gravitated towards the daughter who let her get on with it.'

'What do you mean she rewrote history?' I asked.

Annie raised her eyebrows. I decided that I'd let seventy-plus years be my shield, that I'd shelter under the free pass of an age-related lack of filter allowing a more permissible degree of tactlessness. 'She believed that her marriage to my father was a true love story. That they were soulmates. That their love for each other scaled heights to which other mere mortals could never aspire. Honestly, it was laughable.' Annie turned away, shaking her head as though she was in conversation with her mother.

I waited for her to carry on, but instead she muttered something about needing a shower, leaving me under no illusions that I'd been dismissed in my own home.

I couldn't wait for Marina to get back from visiting her cousin in Sardinia. I needed help working out a suitable plan for this unfathomable woman. She was an odd combination of vulnerable and forthright and, if my instincts didn't suggest otherwise, apparently dismissive of her mother's death.

Unlike Beth, who had seemed terrified that Marina and I would present a challenge that she couldn't accomplish, Annie was like a worker ant who'd run out of leaves to transport. Every time I set foot out of my home, she waylaid me, as though my instructions to take a few days to explore and get her bearings weren't enough. There was something about her that reminded me of Strega as a puppy: full of energy and enthusiasm but not quite sure what the routine was, eager to please and mildly annoying.

Without Marina to bounce off, the undertaking to help women find the missing pieces of themselves seemed less like a fun experiment and more like a serious chore. The unease that

Annie might be here for a cheap extended holiday rather than to overcome a significant trauma started to creep in.

On the third day, I woke early and came out to sit on my terrace, delighting in the quiet and the cooler temperatures of the early hours before the humidity of the recent days hit. Lately, I was remembering our unpredictable British summers with more fondness, the sudden rainy days springing up in periods of sunshine.

A noise from the courtyard dragged me away from my thoughts. A scraping. I peered over the wall and looked down to see Annie in her pyjamas. She was snatching at the spent geraniums in my pots and deadheading the roses with a vigour that bordered on demonic. She flung all the bits onto the cobbles, then grabbed my yard brush and began sweeping, jabbing and stabbing the broom with the energy of a woman who'd been mainlining caffeine. I watched her for a few minutes, trying to comprehend why she would feel the need to be gardening at quarter to six in the morning. An unexpected bonus because, in my book, deadheading fell into the category of doing dull things now in order to have more joy later. Unfortunately, as I'd got older, I was more in the 'joy now, dull things never' mindset, so I didn't often get round to it. Maybe she was one of those tiresome people who saw sleeping as a waste of time. Perhaps she considered anyone who liked to lie in until eight o'clock a lightweight. If my bladder and thoughts would grant me some respite, there was no way I'd be up at this hour. She must have been exhausting to work with.

I crept back to my seat, mulling over this hurricane of a woman. Eventually, I decided that, like a toddler, she needed wearing out, one of those human beings who required constant activity. And even if she didn't, I consoled myself that physical exercise produced endorphins and everyone benefitted from those.

Shortly before seven o'clock, I took her a cup of coffee.

'Morning. You're up bright and early.'

'Once I'm awake, I'm awake.' Almost as an aside, she said, 'I don't like lying there thinking about whether I could have had a better relationship with my mother. Whether my sister will speak to me again.'

I was relieved to catch a glimpse of vulnerability. 'Grief is an unpredictable beast. It floored me when my mother died and I hadn't seen her since my father's funeral, fifteen years earlier. Once I moved here, we hardly had any contact. They didn't own a phone at home until 1983 and I'd already been gone for five years by then. I had to ask the woman from a neighbouring farm to let them know when my daughter Nadia was born.'

A great sadness churned in my chest. It still hurt that they'd never forgiven me, never been the parents I needed at the moment I really needed them. If only they could have held their arms open and reassured me that whatever the world – our tiny Cornish community – thought about me, they were so on my side that they were cheering for Team Veronica. At twenty-seven, I was so young to deal with everything that had happened. I hadn't yet learnt that loyalty could be used as a weapon.

I suddenly became aware of Annie studying me. I must have been going soft in my old age as I felt tears threaten. 'Different times then, anyway,' I said, making the words come out harsh and strong. I was far too ancient to be whining on about what my parents did or didn't get right.

Annie looked down, picking at the plastic hook on the end of the brush. 'It must have been so odd not to have constant contact. No email. No mobile phones. I've messaged my sons every day since I've been here.'

I registered that it was the first time she'd given any indication of how close she was to her children. I felt a flicker of envy that her adult sons tolerated daily interaction. Nadia would simply ignore me if I bombarded her like that. I'd love to have discovered a way of integrating myself more securely in my daughter's life without having to go the whole hog and have her living opposite me.

I continued my story. 'It was like starting a whole new life, really, leaving behind everything that had gone before. We wrote letters in the beginning.' I paused as I remembered the thrill of finding a little blue airmail letter in the postbox, then the disappointment of finding whole paragraphs about the farm, the cows, Mrs Norman's trouble with her waterworks but nothing about the questions I wanted answered. Could they forgive me? Did they still love me?

'Did your mum and dad mind you moving out here?' Annie asked.

'They were farmers. They were too busy to dwell on it.' I had no idea if that was the answer. At the time, I thought they didn't care at all, that they were glad I was disappearing. We weren't a family that spoke openly. Instead we watched the bonds between us twist and fray until inevitably they snapped and released us in our different directions.

Annie wasn't going to let it go. 'They must have put pressure on you to come home at some point? Did they visit?'

I made my tone light. 'My mother came out on a coach all the way from England when Nadia was born in 1981.' I said it as though she'd battled land and sea to reach us, simultaneously shaking away the memory of watching my mother cuddling and soothing Nadia from the doorway of her room. There was hope for the future, love in her face, delight I didn't realise she was capable of. Then her looking up, her expression closing in on itself. *'I hope she has an easier life than yours.'* My mother's disappointment had furled around the room like a November fog, freezing any two-way dialogue, any apology and acceptance.

Annie tilted her head on one side, suggesting she had many more questions up her sleeve.

I'd said enough. I clapped my hands. 'If you're ready for it, I suggest you explore further afield. I'm going to send you to London.'

Although I'd wanted to tease her a little, Annie looked so confused and upset that I rushed in with my explanation.

'Not that London, obviously. *Piccola Londra*. Little London. It's such an odd anomaly – it's a street built in a very British style, with gardens and steps up to the front door, a bit like you'd see in Chelsea or the posh parts of Kensington. I used to go when I first moved here and was feeling homesick for England, wondering whether I should have moved to London instead.'

Annie stuck out her bottom lip. 'That sounds interesting. I'm up for anything. Can I walk there?'

I nodded. 'It's on the other side of the river, north of here, in the Flaminio district.' It would take her a good hour or so to get there and with Marina due back early afternoon after a week away, I wanted to catch up with her without an audience. 'I've got a street map you can borrow.'

Annie's eyes widened and she said, 'Thank you, but I'll use the map on my phone,' as though I'd suggested she washed her clothes in the Tiber and wrung them out with my mangle.

I decided to refrain from sharing my opinion that in twenty years' time, no one would know whether Rome was north or south of Milan because they'd always be following some stupid blue dot instead of looking at the bigger picture.

Annie gestured at her pyjamas. 'I'll sort myself out and head off before it gets too hot.' She paused. 'Thank you. Being here is just the tonic I needed.'

I wasn't sure whether to welcome or dread Marina's verdict on this enigma of a woman.

6

I was constantly in awe of Marina's ability to pull off her helpless old woman act to persuade the most querulous cab drivers to open doors and carry her luggage right up to the top floor. They didn't know her like I did – quite capable of shoving aside any teenager blocking the pavement – 'You're a better door than a window' – or peering over her glasses and frightening even the surliest waiter into speed. Even though she brought her own brand of dominance to the apartment block, if my knees had allowed for it, I would have skipped down the steps to greet her.

We hugged like teenagers reunited after the whole summer holidays rather than separated for a week. 'Did you have a good time?' I asked as she settled down in my kitchen.

The question was rhetorical as Marina never told me about things that went well – 'Happy times don't make interesting stories.'

She wiped her forehead with a handkerchief and dug into her handbag for a fan. I busied about making lunch and relaxing into our routine of Marina holding court at my table while I chopped, diced and spiced.

'It was nice to be beside the sea, of course, and still not too busy, but Rosalia...' As she said her cousin's name, she did an exaggerated intake of breath. 'Her cooking. I must be four kilos lighter.' She gestured to her torso, which, as far as I could see, still had a bosom every bit as heaving as before she left. 'She decided that we – she meant me – needed to cut back on everything. Not a single *biscotto* with my morning cappuccino. Always having to comment on everything. "Marina, not so much salt." "Marina, surely not another glass of wine?"'

She pursed her lips. 'Honestly, this heart of mine could carry me off at any time. And if it does, I'm not bowing out without a good Vermentino in my hand. Also, her house wasn't clean at all. I needed the alcohol in my blood to sanitise the germs.'

I listened patiently through her litany of complaints – the lumpy mattress that meant she'd now have to spend the rest of the summer seeing the osteopath, the cat that pulled a thread on her cashmere jumper, the neighbour practising the piano at all hours.

She finished up with a logic that only Marina could deliver. 'Anyway, I'm going back for another week at the end of September, to celebrate the festival of San Michele.'

For the moment, I was just so glad she was back to help me work out how to channel Annie's phenomenal energy.

She clapped her hands as though she'd delivered the main headline news and she was now ready to switch to the less weighty and light-hearted snippets of local news, i.e. what was happening in my life. 'So, what's new here?' she asked, as though I couldn't possibly compete with the lumpy mattress drama.

'Annie arrived.'

Marina threw her hands up in the air. 'I was waiting for you to tell me about her. What's she like?'

I didn't point out that I knew she'd forgotten. Marina would never admit to that. At most, she'd hiss through her teeth and say something maddening such as, 'Well, you speak about so many things of little consequence, you can't blame me if my brain calls a halt to what it absorbs.'

I described Annie and how she'd probably seen more of Rome in three days than I did in my first five years. 'She's one of those people who does everything at speed, even if there's no need to hurry. There's something frantic, urgent about her. I do wonder if all this getting up at the crack of dawn and walking miles is an effort to block out any thinking.'

'Maybe,' Marina said. 'But how do we get her to confront things if she doesn't want to?'

I was sure Marina would find a means, though it wouldn't be pretty.

Outside, I heard the gates grind open, the patter of Annie's footsteps, the groan of the front door, then the echo of her feet flying along with a nimbleness of knee and hip that Marina and I now lacked.

'Would you like to meet Annie now?'

Quick as a flash, Marina whipped her lipstick out of her handbag and applied it without needing to use a mirror.

I went into the hallway and called Annie.

She came rushing in, a cotton maxi dress billowing behind her in a cloud of white and orange. She presented herself in a way I'd never mastered but often envied. She gave the impression she was dressing solely to please herself. There was an innate insouciance that lent verve to whatever she wore. The mere fact of not caring what anyone else thought was almost a style in itself, so much more striking than a careful matching of accessories, textures and colours.

Marina's expression brightened with the satisfaction of spotting someone who might share her love of jackets, of shoes, of shopping. 'Well, aren't you the breath of fashionable sunshine? That's a very good colour on you.'

Annie smiled. 'Thank you.'

Marina extended her hand, sitting straight-backed and aristocratic like a ruler granting an audience with her subject. The rest of the world might be jostling for supremacy, but there would never be any doubt about the pecking order at Villa Alba. After Strega, of course.

Marina peered at Annie. 'I gather it's been a difficult few months.'

Annie nodded. 'Onwards and upwards.' Again, that air of indifference.

I waved them through to the sitting room, while I busied about making fresh lemonade in the kitchen. I couldn't quite catch all the nuances of the conversation, but I detected a certain level of frustration in Marina's voice, with brief responses from Annie. I took in the tray just as Marina was doing her eyebrow thing.

'Forgive me, Annie, but when you applied to come out here, I understood that there was a certain level of turmoil around your mother's death and your sister's reaction to it.'

'In so far as my mother and I didn't like each other and now it's too late to do anything about it. It's quite shocking to recognise that the person who was supposed to love me actually didn't rate me much at all.'

Even Marina leaned towards disbelief, as though only truly wicked people didn't love their kids. 'Was she really that bad?'

'That's a question I keep asking myself. My sister thinks I was too quick to find fault in her. But then again, I believe she encouraged my mum in her self-delusion.' She put on a country bumpkin accent. 'Nowt so queer as folk.'

Marina folded her arms. 'So you're at a stalemate and you're not willing to do anything about it?'

'What can I do? She sees things one way, I see them another. I'm not going to lie and tell her she's right. I'm hoping that she'll realise that some of Mum's behaviour was totally illogical.' I admired Annie for not backing down at Marina's judgemental tone.

'So basically you're planning to sit here for three months waiting for someone else to change their strongly held opinions?'

I almost spluttered into my drink. Marina would glue herself to an armchair until she died in order to prove that she'd been right all along.

Annie furrowed her brow. 'To be honest, I wanted a break from feeling so confused and thought a complete change would shift something in the right direction – either I'd view things differently or my sister would.'

Marina sniffed. 'You might need to be more proactive than that.'

I regretted voicing my concerns to Marina so soon. After all the years of living with her outspokenness, I still experienced a surge of fear that a huge scene was about to ensue.

'Marina,' I said, 'maybe all Annie needs is some time away from her normal commitments to process what's happened.'

Annie held up her hand. 'You don't need to defend me, Ronnie.' Her tone contained a thread of suppressed emotion, but I couldn't judge whether that was tears or fury. She turned to Marina. 'I'm sorry you've concluded that I'm not making any effort to sort my life out.' She swallowed and her voice, when she spoke again, carried an unmistakable tremble of outrage. 'I can't trust what I think I know about the family, let alone the vision my mother and sister present about the past. I've never been able to make sense of it and, at this point, I'm not sure what's real and what I've half-remembered or even invented.'

Marina's face lit up with rampant curiosity.

I was still corralling my expression into one of polite interest, whereas the temptation was to lean forward, elbows on my knees, and drill right down into the nitty-gritty of the differences between her recollections and the rest of her family's.

Without any prompting, Annie continued. 'If I ever tried to ask Mum about the past, times when she threatened to leave my dad and take us to live in America or disappeared herself for several weeks – I'm sure I'm not making that up – she'd just burst into tears. Her favourite response was, "I don't know what you mean," followed by "I can't talk about your father, I miss him so much." My sister allowed her to maintain that charade right up until when my mother passed away. She even insisted on Mum being buried next to him.'

I felt a sense of panic, of stirring up real pain for Annie, without the skills to guide her through it. It was going to take more than suggesting the best place to watch the sunset over Rome to sieve through that pile of baggage. I glared at Marina, who was capable of blundering in with an accurate assessment of the situation without weighing up whether this was the perfect opportunity to mention it.

I deflected the possibility with my own question. 'Were you close to your sister when you were younger?'

Annie's eyes filled. I'd obviously managed to stick my finger right on the family pressure point. 'We've been close for most of our lives actually. Everyone loves my sister, not just me. She always goes with the flow, floating along on the surface of everything so everyone finds her a delight to be around. Mum loved spending time with her because they would go to the theatre and fancy craft markets at National Trust properties. She allowed Mum to wallow in this fantasy of her perfect husband, our marvellous father.'

She pulled a tissue out of her sleeve. 'Though when it came to sorting out my mum's house, dealing with her finances, the holes in the roof, and her care when she was ill, my sister was nowhere to be seen. I had to help Mum make some difficult decisions, or latterly, more or less force them upon her. Especially when it became clear she couldn't cope on her own any more.' Annie's voice snagged, the way it does when a hurtful memory you thought you'd tamed breaks through the surface like a diver gasping for air. 'She always accused me of being a troublemaker.'

Marina sniffed. 'It's easy not to be a troublemaker if you basically do the ha-ha hee-hee bits but never actually take any responsibility for sorting stuff out. I'm making a bet you're the oldest?'

Annie nodded.

Marina put her hand out and patted Annie's knee. 'I, too, am the oldest. I have two brothers and one sister and my mother always called me the *piantagrane*, the troublemaker. In reality, I consider myself to be a person who sticks to the truth. Which, I am sorry to discover, so many people find unacceptable if it contrasts with the lies they have told themselves.'

Relief washed over Annie's face at Marina's about-turn from accuser to ally. Although Marina's confrontational methods still scared me to death, I felt as though we had something to work with, a little insight into Annie's world. In her story was a splinter that would require some teasing out at a later date. I doubted that many families fell into the Janet and John stereotypes that were embedded in the DNA of my generation growing up. I certainly didn't recall being prepared for a world where mothers fell out with their daughters.

As I sat half-listening to Annie and Marina comparing hard-done-by oldest-sibling stories, I was asking myself if, right at this moment, Nadia was recounting her upbringing to a puzzled audience over in England. '*She was estranged from her own parents, she has a history of falling out with people.*' A portrayal of a woman who didn't notice that her husband was having an affair and then blamed her daughter for not telling her. Which could be a fair assessment, I supposed. Except it didn't *feel* like that.

And it certainly wasn't what I explained to my friends when asked why Nadia had moved to England shortly after

Matteo died. I'd laugh, light-heartedly, acting the libertarian English mother who was completely cool with her only child living in another country. 'It's better for her to be in England, away from the constant reminders of her father. And she has much better job opportunities.'

But the truth was our anger – no longer articulated out loud but still crackling across the airwaves like static in a storm – made close proximity impossible. Then, out of the blue, a year and a half after she'd left, she called to say she'd married Grant – a man I'd never met and was barely aware of – on Matteo's birthday as a tribute to him. I'd always considered myself a non-needy, non-judgemental mother, but informing me after the wedding with an airy 'we got married in a registry office with a couple of friends, spur of the moment' pushed our already strained relations to a place I wasn't sure they'd invented return transport from.

I'd congratulated her in the steadiest voice I could muster, my body shaking with upset that my daughter had excluded me from the one ritual to which most parents could take an invitation for granted. If she wanted me to understand that she hadn't forgiven me, I'd received the message loud and clear.

I spent countless middle-of-the-night hours wondering whether it would ever be possible to make proper, genuine peace. I concluded that my big crime was that I never went digging for bad news, adopting a view that trouble would find me soon enough. History had taught me that. I'd been afraid to tug at the thread of my marriage in case everything else unravelled – and I wasn't sure I could knit life back together for a second time. So I did what I needed to survive – I shut my eyes and ears. I was a coward. Which provided a magnificent dilemma. I could give Nadia the benefit of the doubt and assume she had sensed my weakness and made a misguided attempt to protect me. Or I could believe she'd justified chucking me under the marital bus because she despised my lack of courage.

Whichever it was, I hadn't covered myself in maternal glory. I didn't know whether I'd ever have the opportunity to rectify that. Yet my contrary heart still resisted throwing caution to the wind and allowing her to take up residence at Villa Alba. Logic played no part in love.

7

Unlike Beth, who had dutifully carried out her challenges without involving us, Annie craved our company. She enjoyed sparring with Marina, which suggested a certain robustness of spirit. Marina, for her part, was the perkiest she'd been in months, challenging Annie's assertion that she dressed for herself, rather than to attract male interest.

'But surely you like to be noticed? Doesn't it put a little spring in your step when a man compliments you on what you're wearing or remarks on a new haircut?' Marina insisted.

Annie pulled a face. 'I hope my hair and my clothes won't be the first thing anyone focuses on.'

'You say that, but I don't believe you. You dress in a way that demands attention,' Marina said.

They could spend an hour batting their views backwards and forwards. How showing a bit of cleavage could facilitate good service (Marina). How women would never get the respect they deserved if they relied on their bodies rather than their brains (Annie). Often enough Strega and I hopped on my Vespa and left them to it.

Nearly a fortnight into Annie's stay, Marina – who usually

refused to go out during the day between May and August on the grounds of the heat – announced: 'I'm going to the Borghetto Flaminio market on Sunday with Annie to help her find some vintage bargains.'

Annie smiled. 'Would you like to come, Ronnie?' She quickly rushed in with, 'If you have nothing better to do.'

'That's kind of you, but this is Marina's territory. I don't have a good eye for second-hand things.'

Marina frowned. 'Of course you'll join us.'

'I'd really like you to,' Annie said.

There was something compelling about this woman. Everything about her was so contradictory. Despite her outward bravado, I sensed her insecurity, the sort that came from never being certain that people enjoyed your company, a hankering for reassurance that an invitation thrown open casually did include her. It was a total contrast to the confidence that Marina had that not only was she invited, but any social event hinged on her availability. Yet there was a resilience about Annie, an irrepressible spirit. She had an optimistic disposition, the sort that couldn't be taught, that surged up despite the evidence that life could be tough, unfair and unrewarding. Apart from that one occasion when she'd talked about her sister being her mother's favourite, she'd warded off any further questions with 'It is what it is.'

I didn't feel she was entirely convinced, or if she was, she hadn't found a way to walk the walk. I wondered if she'd be better off flying home to patch things up sooner rather than later, instead of allowing her sister's fury to ferment. Time apart had simply entrenched Nadia and me more firmly into opposing positions. I wasn't sure whether that might be the same for Annie. There was an intensity about her that my mother would have described as 'still waters running deep'. Sometimes I caught her staring at me, her brow wrinkling as though she was sieving through everything I said and weighing up whether she believed me. I found it both annoying and disconcerting.

Most of the time, however, she brought energy to our sun-baked days, and despite my determination to keep my distance, I sought Annie out. I couldn't understand how any mother hadn't adored her. Disloyally, I considered how much more harmonious my relationship might have been with Nadia if she'd greeted my suggestions – days out, food to try, friends to invite – with a 'why not?' attitude. I'd spent a large part of my life chasing after Nadia as she fluttered away, putting forward ideas for things we might enjoy together. Eventually, I'd run out of energy to scatter breadcrumbs in the hope that the trail would lead back to me.

Annie, on the other hand, was happy to join me on mundane errands. 'Gives me an insight into how people live here.' She'd cling onto me on the back of the Vespa when I went to the supermarket, swearing loudly if a taxi cut me up. She reserved her most ear-splitting shriek for the time I blocked a teenage boy-racer in a minicar – little more than a golf cart – who thought he could push in front of an old *nonna* on a Vespa. My British sense of orderly queuing and turn-taking had survived Italianisation. As had my dual belief that no fourteen-year-old should be allowed on Rome's roads in anything motorised and it was a rite of passage for all teenagers to know the delights of waiting for a bus in the rain.

'What's the story with these funny little cars?' Annie had asked, peeling herself off the back of the bike.

'Very good question. There's a theory that they're safer than mopeds – they're not supposed to go faster than about thirty miles an hour, but, of course, the kids find ways to soup them up. They're a popular fourteenth-birthday present because they don't need a licence.'

'Fourteen? Fourteen?! Driving on the main roads in a

capital city?' Annie had looked as though she'd never heard such a nonsensical idea.

When I made comments like that, Marina teased me about being 'so Anglo-Saxon', but it was reassuring that I wasn't alone in thinking that anyone who still relied on their mother to buy spot cream shouldn't be playing chicken with the bus to the Vatican.

Over the four decades I'd been in Rome, Italy's lip-service to rules in theory versus blatant disregard in reality both attracted and repelled me. I applauded the rebellion, the insistence of living in the moment, the sheer chutzpah of finding inventive excuses why that particular piece of legislation didn't apply now, to that person. But there was no escaping how often that headbutted against my sense of doing the right thing for the right thing's sake.

I couldn't deny that I enjoyed having Annie as an ally against Marina's lawlessness. After all this time, I still died inside at how she pushed to the front of queues, flapping her fingers at anyone who dared to protest. Her bare cheek as she scoffed up samples of cheese, ham and olives at market stalls without ever feeling obliged to make a reciprocal purchase. And that was before I wanted to crawl under the table if – God forbid – a restaurant meal wasn't to her satisfaction.

Against my better judgement, when Sunday rolled around, I found myself whizzing off in a cab to be the bag and sunhat holder while those two searched for bargains at the market. Marina had set Annie the challenge of buying an item that she would have dismissed as mutton dressed as lamb back in the UK. Or, 'as we say in Italy, "*dietro liceo, davanti museo*" – "from behind, the school; from the front, the museum"'. Marina had never subscribed to age dictating the length of skirts or the extent of cleavage, and somehow, she pulled it off.

My goodwill faded within about fifteen minutes as they riffled through the rails of 'vintage' clothes. If that moth-eaten coat was worth fifty euros, Marina and I merely had to empty our wardrobes to dine on lobster for the rest of our lives. I sat at the café while Marina and Annie tried on hats bedecked with ribbons and feathers and sifted through jewellery that all looked the same to me. But Marina had a knack for homing in on the one gem in a sea of tat and picking out a brooch that revived an old jacket.

Annie resisted the forcefulness of Marina's opinions with a fortitude that had sometimes failed me. Now and then, I'd given into pussy bows and frills that were at odds with my penchant for tie-dye. Annie did, however, embrace Marina's insistence that 'You can wear anything as long as you do it with enough pizzazz.' Miniskirts, leopard-skin tops, lace bodices were bartered over and snapped up for a song, pushing Annie right up the leaders' board in Marina's affections. 'You're a woman of discerning taste.' I didn't voice the fact that what she'd bought called to mind the Moulin Rouge burlesque shows I'd seen in Paris.

By the time we made it home, Marina had nodded off and as we drew into the driveway, she was snoring lightly, though immediately denied falling asleep when I shook her awake. 'I was resting my eyes. The sun has dried them out.' I knew better than to argue or to help her out of the car. 'I'm nearly eighty, not a hundred and five!'

I left her pursing her lips with determination not to ask for a hand up as she levered herself to her feet, hanging onto the car door and leaning heavily on her stick. Instead, I pulled Annie's leg about her purchases. 'If you're not careful, when you arrive back in England, you'll curse yourself for buying a whole load of stuff that needed a dose of Roman sunshine and the smell of pasta puttanesca wafting on the summer air to retain its magic.'

Annie grinned. 'At the very least, every time I look at that red Afghan coat, I'll have a little laugh to myself about Marina winkling a marriage proposal out of her second husband by turning up to his office in something similar with nothing under-neath. She's got some balls, that woman.'

'She certainly has.' I didn't add my own belief that the type of men who were spurred to commitment by a flagrant appeal to sexuality might not exhibit the same staying power for the poor-er/in sickness vows of marriage.

A bit of the day's hilarity seeped away as the memory of Gianna at Matteo's funeral, all film-star hat, veil and loud but elegant tears, trespassed into my mind. For the hundredth time, I reminded myself that it wasn't her glamour that took him away. It was her willingness to make him the focus of her whole life. At least according to what she had said when – despite my instructions to ignore her if she had the gall to turn up – Marina had confronted her outside the church. I was too numb to inter-vene but not so out of it that I couldn't hear her yelling that I was a buttoned-up Englishwoman incapable of giving her husband the love he deserved.

I tried never to think about the debacle that followed. Nadia's rage that I hadn't controlled Marina – as if 'control' was a word that could even squeeze into the same context as her. These days, I chose – as far as possible – not to dwell on anything to do with Matteo.

With a deliberate redirecting of my thoughts, I pushed open the courtyard gate to my private garden, beckoning to Annie to help me choose a spot for the Buddha statue I'd bought at the market. I jumped. There in the corner, under the shade of the olive tree, sat a woman. A woman with swollen ankles propped up on my bench and an even bigger stomach. The unmistakable bloom of pregnancy. My daughter.

The fear that I'd get it wrong, that I'd burst out with the thought uppermost in my mind, 'But I didn't think you wanted children,' paralysed me, stopped me even acknowledging that she was clearly expecting a baby. 'Nadia! What are you doing here? Why didn't you let me know you were coming? Is Grant with you?' I asked, the questions pouring out of me.

Nadia's responses were quiet and gentle – 'I was homesick for Rome', 'Grant couldn't get the time off' – but still no reference to the bigger issue that was burning brightly. I was wary of deluding myself by finding her conciliatory. I wanted to hug her, to do that annoying thing of touching her bump, to ask her if the baby was kicking, when it was due. But I'd lost confidence in my maternal instincts, afraid that anything I did would be misconstrued as critical or nosey or negative.

To my astonishment, everything in me rejoiced. I wondered how on earth we'd been reduced to one frosty visit a year when the burst of pleasure in my heart underlined that I loved her beyond anything that Matteo and his mistress could taint. But old habits died hard.

I squeezed her shoulder and said, 'Well, what a wonderful surprise. It's lovely to see you.'

I introduced Annie, who said a perfunctory hello and disappeared with a haste bordering on rude.

Marina showed no such tact, tapping over to her and leaning in for a hug. 'Hello, you. This is a turn-up for the books.' She pointed the silver top of her cane at Nadia's stomach. 'Ha. See you bottled it at the exit to last-chance saloon. Your mother will be delighted.' She winked. 'If you need to dip the dummy in whisky, you know where I am.'

I swatted at Marina. 'No one gives a baby whisky any more. You'd be had up for child abuse.'

I looked at Nadia's face, trying to piece together all the many parts of the picture that made no sense – a heavily pregnant daughter, one who'd always been vociferous in her desire to remain childless, here without warning. I had far more questions than immediate answers.

She swung her feet down from the bench. I braced myself for her announcing that she was going up for a lie-down, my wait for clues doomed to stretch out into the evening. Instead, she said, 'I'm moving back to Rome for the foreseeable future. I need to make plans.'

I couldn't resist a snatched image of pushing my grandchild in a pram with random passers-by peering in and saying admiringly, '*Che bello! Carino!*'

But something in her tone carried a warning. I shouldn't take it for granted that I formed part of Nadia's plans.

8

Tears followed the delivery of Nadia's bombshell. She brushed at her face. 'Baby hormones are getting to me.'

Marina said under her breath, 'Wait till you're up all night.'

I glared at her and she had the good grace to look sheepish. I was surprised Marina had been so welcoming. Despite my pleas for peace, she had remained furious about Nadia stepping in to defend Gianna at Matteo's funeral.

Since then, on the rare occasions Nadia had come to visit, Marina had entertained herself by throwing inflammatory comments into the conversation, gleefully warming her hands on the resulting bonfire. She thought Nadia's views on every-thing – Matteo, Gianna, never mind climate change, vegetari-anism and the fur trade – needed a little correction. Everything about Marina was contradictory. She enjoyed goading Nadia and Grant, relishing the mischief-making, but only if I was prepared to play the straight guy. It unsettled her that Nadia and I were at odds with each other – 'You're so stubborn. Have it out with her and move on. What are you waiting for? Some stupid deathbed coming together?'

Now, sooner than I'd anticipated, fate had provided a golden opportunity to build some bridges, while also delivering the unexpected bonus of a grandchild. I suggested to Marina with a tilt of my head that she left us to it. Her FOMO had her flashing pleading looks at me, but I stood firm and she eventually plodded off.

Nadia lay down on the garden swing chair and I sat opposite, rubbing my hands on my knees and rehearsing the many variations of 'So what *is* the plan?' I tried to alight on a format that would sound welcoming, interested, open to understanding what had brought her here but, equally, not pressuring her before she was ready. I didn't manage to find the words. Instead, I said, 'Would you like some iced water?'

Nadia shook her head. 'Aren't you even going to ask me *why* I've come back?'

That familiar 'playing darts blindfold' sensation rushed through me. 'I was afraid of prying, darling. I wanted you to tell me in your own time.'

Nadia pressed her fingers into her eyes as though I was the most hopeless mother ever. When she finally looked at me, she said, 'The baby wasn't planned. We never wanted children. Except I've changed my mind and Grant hasn't. I'm on my own with this.'

Nadia's cheeks puffed out and I was reminded of how she used to hold her breath as a little girl when she was trying not to cry.

Every instinct in me yearned to calm and soothe her. 'Maybe he'll come round when the baby arrives, love. Sometimes the idea is frightening – it's such a huge change for everyone – but when the baby is actually here, he might see it differently.'

Nadia raised her chin. I knew how unforgiving she could be. If I hadn't carried her in my own body for nine months, I would have sworn she was Marina's daughter. 'No. No. I will never trust a man who tried to force me to have an abortion.

Nothing even vaguely approaching, "Whatever you want to do, I'll support you." Not good enough.'

I gasped at the idea of Grant attempting to persuade Nadia to opt for a termination. My frequent irritation with Nadia's stubbornness melted into gratitude that my daughter knew her own mind and could stand up for herself.

It took everything I'd learnt since Matteo's death not to leap into a diatribe about Grant's shortcomings. It was so tempting to let rip about that aura he had of knowing better than everyone else on any topic you cared to mention, then taking it as a personal affront if you dared to disagree. I knew from experience that Marina badmouthing my dead husband with such regularity did nothing to salve my hurt. In fact, it had the opposite effect of making me feel an utter fool for spending thirty-seven years married to such a cad. I played it safe and stuck to practicalities. 'So where do you stand in terms of custody for the baby?'

'I won't even bother telling him when he or she is born.'

I couldn't help wondering whether the ability to carry out a scorched-earth strategy ran through our DNA, given how completely I'd cut myself off from my parents. Still, it was no more than Grant deserved.

'I've renovated one of the other apartments since you were last here but Annie is living in it at the moment. Zia Laura's old place is empty, though,' I said, brushing aside any misgivings about Nadia living next door. A child changed everything. I wasn't sure that Nadia had ever picked up a baby before or spent any time with young children. Without my mother-in-law, I'd have found the responsibility of caring for a newborn overwhelming.

Nadia frowned. 'But you don't want me to live in it?'

I jumped up. 'No, no. That's not what I'm saying at all. I'm offering it to you so we can help when the baby's born. Beth, our previous guest, stayed there for ten weeks, so I know everything is in working order.'

It killed me to see the mistrust on Nadia's face, her eyes narrowing as she weighed up the motives behind my proposal. How differently I would have reacted if I'd known she was pregnant last December when she'd first mooted the idea of an extended stay in Rome this spring. It was miraculous how all my misgivings were dissolving in the face of the opportunity to be a proper grandma.

She gazed at me defiantly. 'I'm thinking of renting somewhere near the Parco degli Acquedotti.'

'That's on the other side of the city! That could easily take an hour on the metro.' I paused, to get my filter in place. Emotion never won the day with Nadia. Only logic. Always logic. 'And anyway, you'd have to sign a contract for four years, wouldn't you?'

'Yes.'

I kept a neutral face while allowing my heart to do a high-kick at the idea of tying her to Rome for four years. Time for a tiny baby to grow into a young child who, with a bit of luck, would form a strong and lasting attachment to Nonna Ronnie. The triumphant dance in my head would have looked like a drunken and raucous rendition of Strip the Willow at a Scottish wedding if I'd acted it out.

'I'll make sure there's a break clause so I can give six months' notice,' she said.

Of course. There would always be an escape route away again. My mind responded with an image of me sobbing against an airport window, watching as a jet bound for England left a white trail across the sky. I already wanted to throw myself on the floor and lock onto her ankles. Keep it casual, Ronnie.

'But you're planning to settle here for a while?' I rushed to add, 'Initially, at least?' so she couldn't accuse me of pressurising her.

Nadia nodded. 'I'm on maternity leave for a year, but I've got the option of doing a three-day week from home later on. I'd probably have to go back to England for one meeting a month. I'll figure it out.'

'You'll need childcare.'

'I'll work when the baby sleeps.'

I was so glad Marina wasn't there to let slip how I'd said the same thing before Nadia was born and, within weeks, she'd found me sobbing into my dictionaries while rocking Nadia in a bouncy chair with my foot.

Never before had the phrase 'slowly slowly catchee monkey' reverberated so loudly in my brain. 'Well, the offer's there if you'd like to move next door temporarily and see how it goes after the baby is born.'

Nadia looked relieved. 'I had forgotten how hot Rome is in the summer. It's probably not the best time to run around flat-hunting. Especially not at this point.' She gestured to her bump.

'When is the baby due?' I asked, as though I was playing some mad maternal game of What's the Time, Mister Wolf?

'In four weeks. The ninth of July. Today was the very last day I could fly.'

Nadia's face defied me to panic, to splutter questions about medical notes and maternity units and routes to hospital. I didn't fall into the trap. I smiled and said, 'I'm so glad you came. How about I make up the bed in the spare room and we'll get you moved into the other apartment in due course?'

Despite my fears that Nadia would flit out of my life again before I'd proved my value as a babysitter, I took some fresh linen from the armoire in my bedroom. Grinning into the mirror, I did an elated dance, waving my fists at my reflection and mouthing, 'I'm going to be a grandma.'

Maybe this would be my chance to start afresh and be the mother I'd hoped to be, with a bonus opportunity to not balls it up as a grandmother.

9

Fowey 1973

On my twenty-fifth birthday, I could not shake the feeling that I was living the wrong life. The day before, Eddie had told me he wasn't coming back to Cornwall again for another three weeks – 'You know the run-up to Christmas is mad at work.' He'd pulled out a roll of notes. 'Here, you make the house beautiful. Choose a really big tree, buy the girls all those Sindy dolls they like and get a decent turkey – order from that farmer over near Looe.'

'Can't I come to London with you? I'd love to see all the Christmas lights. I don't want to sit here all alone on my birthday.'

Initially, he'd pulled me close. 'Darling, you know I want to take you with me, but you'd be a distraction,' he said, his hands sweeping across my body. I got a buzz out of how attractive this clever, successful man still found me, two years into our relationship. How much he loved me despite all the naysayers.

I tried a different tack. 'I wouldn't get in your way. I could help with the girls when they're not at their mother's. I could cook dinner, look after you.' I knew I sounded like a ten-year-old begging to be allowed to stay up late on New Year's Eve, but the dark winter nights were so long on my own, day after day. To begin with, I'd relished the freedom of having a whole house to myself that first summer when I'd moved in as a housekeeper. But by autumn, our relationship had moved on to a different level and we couldn't keep our hands off each other. My entire existence revolved around when Eddie would be able to escape London and return to me again.

Now, a couple of years on, I wanted more from Eddie. There was only so much *Are You Being Served?* and *Some Mothers Do 'Ave 'Em* that I could stand. Eddie encouraged me to invite my friends round while simultaneously making me feel ashamed of them – 'I'm surprised you get on so well with Linda. She's not the brightest spark, is she?' Or if I said Rosemary was coming over: 'The thing is, Veronica, if you surround yourself with – how shall I put it? – unambitious people, you'll probably end up like them. Law of averages really.'

Over time, I'd let things slide, making excuses not to go out with the gang I'd grown up with and gradually not bothering to phone them. So at this point, I didn't feel as though I could say, 'Please come round and eat cake with me on my birthday.' I'd considered myself so mature, superior even, with my older boyfriend, my big house with the sea view, weekends with my adopted family, playing at being a stepmother to Eddie's girls. I didn't know how to admit that I was secretly envious of my friends, bundling around each other's houses on a Saturday night with cans of Harp lager and bottles of Martini and their silly drunken games of Twister.

Eddie put his hands in his pockets and rocked back on his heels. 'The girls are staying with Nancy at the moment so they can be with us over Christmas. Three short weeks, darling. It will go quickly.'

I sighed. 'I know. I just thought I'd have a decent job at this stage, especially now the UK has joined the European Economic Community. I expected there to be loads of translating work. Did you talk to your friend who imports from the Champagne region?'

Eddie scowled. 'I told you, everyone's flat out until Christmas. In the new year, I'll go through my contacts.' He tweaked my nose. 'Be patient. These things don't happen overnight.'

'You've been saying that for the last six months.' The words slipped out before I could stop them.

Eddie's head flew round and he took a step closer, a pulse throbbing in his jaw, his pupils hard and dark. He put his face so close to mine that I could smell the cider he'd had in the pub at lunchtime, mingling with the undertones of Old Spice aftershave. He pointed towards the door. 'If you think you can do better by yourself, why don't you run back to your mum and dad and see how you like getting up at the crack of dawn to sort out those cows. You've got a cushy number here, so stop all the moaning.'

I could feel the urge to fight him, to call his bluff. But my inclination to backpedal, to keep the faith in this intense and powerful love affair, triumphed. And I was too far down this road to contemplate the humiliation of admitting to my parents that their reservations had had substance. 'Sorry. I miss you. I miss the girls. I'd love to take them to Hamleys.' Until I'd met Eddie, I'd been disdainful of the girls I knew from school, pushing prams and saying, 'Lucky you, jetting off to Paris. I wish,' before leaning down to wipe the nose of a snotty toddler or jiggle a baby on their hips. Now, I understood the starburst of pleasure that came from a small hand slipping into mine, a glance to see if I was watching an act of bravery on the hanging bars, the blind confidence that I'd know how God stayed in the sky. I'd never considered myself maternal, but Eddie's daughters had uncovered a side to me I didn't know existed.

Eddie relaxed, his stance softening. He murmured into my hair, 'If I pull in the numbers now, I'll be able to take a bit more holiday in the springtime. I'll take you somewhere special. Paris even.'

I barely managed to hang onto the words, 'I've already spent a year in Paris. I speak fluent French and I want to use it before all I can remember is *un café au lait et un croissant s'il vous plaît.*'

'Thank you,' I said instead. 'That would be lovely.'

But I obviously didn't sound quite grateful enough as his face clouded and he spoke to me in monosyllables for the rest of the evening. I tried to apologise, but he brushed me off, reminding me that he had to set off for London at five a.m. 'Not everyone can sleep in on a Monday morning like you.'

I slept fitfully, lying awake for long periods wanting to cry, childishly disappointed that our row would ruin my birthday.

I got up at half-past four to make him tea and toast, which seemed to mollify him.

He leaned in for a long kiss. 'I've left a present for you on the dining-room table. I need to get on the road now, but I'll ring you when I arrive at the office and you can open it then. I want to hear your reaction to it.' He stood back and gazed at me intently. 'I love you so much.'

The present was small and square and I didn't dare admit what I was hoping for. Eddie was adamant he wouldn't get married again, but lately, I'd made a bit of headway arguing that once his divorce finally came through, it would give the girls more stability. Maybe it would cement in their minds that they could rely on me, unlike their mother, who changed arrangements at the drop of a hat. I wanted to be part of their lives, and we'd grown together. Heather had evolved into a boisterous six-year-old who hadn't yet mastered how to stay out of trouble at school and Lyndsey, now three, didn't even remember a time without me.

From nine o'clock onwards, I hovered around the living-room phone, periodically picking at the edges of the Sellotape, impatient for Eddie's call. I debated what I would say, something witty and fresh, that would mark me out as different from his first wife, that would prove I was his equal, his soulmate. I'd drive over to my mum and dad, take pleasure in proving them wrong, in confounding their assertion that 'a man like that will have his fun, then you'll be used goods and no one else will want you'.

When the phone rang at 9.45 a.m., I jumped.

'Happy birthday, my darling. Go on, then. Open it.'

'I'm nervous,' I said, giggling with anticipation.

I ripped off the paper and opened the box.

'Wow. A diamond bracelet,' I remarked, covering the mouthpiece of the phone to release a little gasp of disappointment. I took a deep breath. 'It's beautiful, thank you.'

'You don't sound very excited. Cost me an arm and a leg, that did. For God's sake, Veronica. What would actually make you happy? You're twenty-five, you've got a diamond bracelet, you're living in a four-bedroomed house by the sea and you're still not satisfied.' He had a way of speaking that made him sound as though he hated me.

My stomach clenched and churned and I fumbled for the right words. 'Sorry, I'm just surprised. I've never had anything with diamonds before.' I cleared my throat. 'I love it. Really.'

His voice was flat as he ended the call. 'Have a good day.'

I sank down onto the settee and cried. Self-loathing enveloped me for my provincial longing to have a ring on my finger, despite the many times I'd waxed lyrical about the tyranny of marriage and the narrow-mindedness of people who still talked about me 'living in sin'. At eighteen, when I'd set off for university, my heart was full of adventure, of bravery, of determination. I knew I'd travel the world, achieve things that I wasn't yet aware even existed. I'd spread my wings beyond far horizons with a nonchalance that would amaze me. Yet here I was, pushing all my ambitions to one side.

My mother rang, imparting her surprise that my 'boyfriend' – an audible filling of the lungs before she articulated the word – hadn't taken a day off work to celebrate my birthday. 'No ring for your finger then?'

There was no running back to my parents. I'd prove them wrong and show them that Eddie was committed to me. How could my dad with his wireless and my mum with her darning understand the fierce passion between Eddie and me that made all the sacrifices worth it? I needed to stop letting their criticisms chip away at our beautiful relationship. So what if I had to give up my idea of zipping off to France, touring vineyards and being the translating lynchpin for big commercial deals? Perhaps I could keep my French up at an evening class. I'd direct my energy towards the girls. I could even teach Heather French; she was bright enough for sure. I was lucky to have found a man who loved me so intensely.

I jiggled the bracelet on my wrist, the diamonds reflecting different colours in the light. It would all be fine. Absolutely fine.

10

Present Day

Nadia had never liked me 'hovering' when she lived at home, but my maternal urge to feed prevailed. I clicked open the door to the spare room and peered in. Nadia raised her head. 'I've brought you some coffee – it's decaf – and fruit.'

She smiled. 'Thank you.'

'Did you sleep well?'

'I did until heartburn woke me up.'

'I had that with you. Your grandmother told me that it was caused by babies who had a lot of hair already. I always thought it was an old wives' tale, but you came out with a shock of dark hair.'

I stopped myself from talking about what a sweet baby she was. How she hated me to put her down. How there were only two people she would go to without screaming so loud she could have interrupted the Papal mass at the Vatican. One was Matteo's mother and, weirdly, the other was Marina, who would hold her in one arm and point a stern finger at her while singing a lullaby of 'Stop this stupid nonsense'. There were times when I was so desperate for someone else to take over that I wouldn't have cared if Marina had been chanting a string of swear words.

'Do you need anything?' I asked instead.

'No thanks. If it's all right with you, I'll move into the other apartment today, unless you've got another middle-aged broken wing flying in?'

I bristled both at her tone and the fact that after one night under my roof she was already chomping at the bit to have her own space. 'No, we're still sifting through applications, so you're in luck.'

Nadia stretched. 'Can you give me the keys, please?'

'I'll help you get settled in.'

'If you don't mind, I'd like to spend some time in there on my own, just suss out the whole vibe without getting distracted.'

Suss out the whole vibe? Nadia had clearly been watching too many films set in California featuring surfers half her age.

I relinquished my fantasy of running between my home and hers, fetching vases, jugs and pictures and positioning them in the perfect place to great approval. I'd imagined making a list of what we still needed and – this was the exciting bit – planning a day out to choose a Moses basket, a cot, some bedding, baby clothes... I'd briefly considered knitting an heirloom cardigan or christening shawl before reminding myself that even before I had arthritis in my thumb, I regularly used to snatch the stitches off my needles in a temper. All things considered, even if I could force my fingers to cooperate, I didn't think Nadia's 'vibe' would be a knitted cardie with teddy bear buttons and I wasn't going to run the risk of witnessing 'the face'.

'That's fine. I'll leave the keys on the table. I'm popping out with Annie this morning anyway. I promised I'd introduce her to my hairdresser so she can get her roots done.'

'Doesn't she know that hair dye leaches through your skin into your blood?'

I'd already been in trouble for my own blue highlights so I tried to sidestep the vanity versus health argument. 'I'm sure she does.'

'But you're happy to facilitate her allowing chemicals to poison her body?'

'I'm happy to let her make her own choices.'

Repeat after me. Do not engage in arguments you cannot win. I would have to drill that bit of wisdom into my frontal cortex when it came to having opinions on how Nadia looked after her baby.

I knocked on Annie's door. 'Still happy to go to the hairdresser's at ten?'

'Yes, looking forward to a transformation. Come in. Give me five minutes to stick a bit of mascara on.'

I wandered out onto her terrace, staring out over the Vatican and still marvelling at how I'd landed here. I wondered how many people ended up in different countries because of love – or the aftermath of love gone wrong elsewhere. Annie was here because of her relationship with her mother. Beth had arrived in our lives because her husband had ditched her for someone else. I'd wound up here because love had carried me to places it was madness to go, with consequences I could never have foreseen.

Annie broke that train of thought. 'Sorry to keep you waiting.'

Nadia was just opening the door to her apartment as we walked down the stairs.

'Morning, Nadia.' Annie was much jollier than she'd been the day before. Perhaps she'd been awkward at stumbling into our family reunion, if my squeezing Nadia on the shoulder could bear such a grand title.

Nadia nodded. 'All right?'

Nadia, at forty-two, was no longer a child I could lecture about manners, despite my temptation to nudge her and hiss, 'Do try to sound vaguely interested.'

Annie, on the other hand, was in full flow as we marched down the hill. 'So where does Nadia live in England? How long is she staying? Is her husband joining her? Are you thrilled she's here?'

Normally, I was very good at keeping my cards close to my chest, but I didn't want Annie to feel in the way – it wasn't her fault that Nadia had popped up out of the blue. I trod a fine line, filling in the basic details about my daughter's life and my hopes and fears surrounding her arrival without homing in on the specifics around Grant in case Nadia got wind that I'd been discussing her private affairs.

'Did you mind that she moved to England?' Annie asked.

'She'd grown up knowing I'd worked in Paris after university, so I'd already planted the idea of living abroad in her mind. I'd cut off completely from England – she barely had any contact with family there, so, unwittingly, I made it a bit of a forbidden fruit. It felt quite natural for her to study over there – she was always an adventurous child, never worried about following the pack. I assumed she was curious about her origins and would get it out of her system while she did her degree.'

A busload of tourists poured out onto the pavement. As we navigated our way around them, I reflected on how easily Annie and I chatted. It was such a contrast to the minefield of my interactions with Nadia.

Clearly my daughter was a source of fascination for Annie, who skirted the throng of visitors and resumed her questioning. 'Has Nadia been in England all that time then? Since university?'

'No. She came back here when she graduated, but London was always a pull for her. When Matteo, her dad, died six years

ago, she felt a change of scene would do her good.' I winced a
little at this extravagant stretch of the truth.

'And you didn't fancy joining her?'

I exhaled as though the idea was preposterous. 'I won't ever
go back there to live.'

'That's very definite. Why not?'

It was such a direct question that the honest answer sprang
to my lips before I located my half-truth. 'I fell in love with the
wrong man when I was young. He had a violent temper. I
stayed too long. Italy gave me a fresh start.'

Annie stared at me with that intensity again. 'Wow. I was
not expecting that as an answer.' She went quiet.

That familiar feeling of shame swept through me. I still had
to work hard to banish the thought that my naivety, my conviction that he was my destiny, had somehow put Eddie under so
much pressure that I caused his despicable behaviour. Guilt
about how things ended still tempted me to make excuses for
the way he'd paralysed me with his vicious tirades; the haranguing, often into the early hours, about needing to grow up, 'to give
it a rest and let me be the judge of how to deal with my stupid
ex-wife'. Even now, angry shouting in the street outside my
home with sturdy ancient walls in between still made my heart
hammer in fear.

I pushed open the door to the hairdresser's, grateful for
the door chime yanking me away from my memories. Giorgio
did his over-the-top welcome, pulling me into a theatrical hug
and exclaiming about how I'd been guzzling the elixir of
youth. I introduced Annie and explained how she wanted her
roots touching up and a trim. He screwed up his face and
demanded that I translate. I'd grown used to the bluntness of
hairdressers, beauticians and shop assistants over the years but
still felt the need to cushion the blow for British sensibilities.
As Giorgio picked up strands of Annie's hair, lifting it away
from her forehead and cheeks, I took a moment to choose how

to convey the 'No. Not a trim. Restyle. All this hair has to go, hiding such a perfectly shaped face. I can make her look twenty years younger. And this dark brown, far too wicked witch.'

'Giorgio's suggesting you go for quite a dramatic chop to showcase your beautiful cheekbones. And perhaps a little lighter?' I ventured.

Giorgio's grasp of English was better than I expected and he launched into a lively discussion with lots of hand waving. He sealed the deal – in his view – 'You want to look like your grandma?'

Annie laughed at the outrageous cheek of the man, brow-beaten into agreement to do whatever he wanted.

He broke off from his creative diatribe to deal with a woman who had come in with her husband. They both talked about what needed to happen to the poor man's thinning hair as though he was one of those plastic doll's heads to be experimented on. On her way out, the woman shouted over her shoulder as an underling led him to the sink – 'Make him look like George Clooney.'

Giorgio responded, 'Then the other women will steal him from you!' and I didn't dare catch the eye of any other female in the salon. I wasn't sure anyone would be rushing to make advances on a man who still needed his wife to instruct his hairdresser.

After checking Annie had logged into the salon's Wi-Fi and had Google Translate on hand if Giorgio got too busy with the scissors, I left her to it. I walked home slowly, pausing to sit in the shade as the midday sunshine speared down its rays. Annie's questions had unsettled me. I'd been too wounded, too proud, to have a frank conversation with my parents regarding how they felt about anything. But also too cowardly, in case what they thought of me was worse than I feared. Instead, I'd run. I'd removed the option of reparation by charging off to

Italy, blockading myself into another country, where all emotions arrived in letters, with a two- to three-week time lag.

Eventually, I heaved myself to my feet, admitting what I'd never allowed myself to think. My pride, my own hurt had made it nearly impossible for my parents to apologise. It was far easier to blame them for our estrangement, to bestow evil traits upon them, than to risk accepting that I'd had a part to play. But it was too late for us.

I flirted with the notion of sitting Nadia and Marina down – Annie too, if I was going for broke – and peeling the layers back. That twenty-seven-year-old woman still lodging in my heart held the key to lifting my lifelong burden. I toyed with the idea of saying it all out loud and watching everyone's faces melt into disbelief.

That would require a courage I didn't have. No one at the age of seventy-four needed to busy themselves poking sleeping dogs awake.

11

Annie knocked on my door in the early afternoon and did a shy 'Ta-da!'

My hands flew to my face. 'You're a completely different person!' Her shoulder-length hair hung in tousled blonde waves with some streaks of copper. 'Giorgio's made you look as though you've forgotten your surfboard somewhere!'

Annie laughed and said, 'It's a long time since I've been near a surfboard. Decades, in fact.' I watched her expression drift as though she'd disappeared into a memory. She often gave the impression that the past was washing over her, trapping her in an endless tussle between things it was too late to change and those that she hadn't yet worked out how to solve going forwards.

'Well, you'd fit in perfectly now. Do you like it? Those colours make your eyes look so blue. I hadn't realised how stunning they are.'

Annie ran her fingers through her hair, and delight flashed over her features. 'I love it. I feel like this is who I was meant to be. My sister has been telling me for years that I should chop it all off.'

'Why don't you send her a photo? I'm assuming she knows you're here? A non-threatening offering of an olive branch?'

'I'll think about it,' she said.

I recognised that same procrastination tool I'd often used. The thinking about it that translated into 'I will barricade that idea into a dark compartment in my mind and wait for it to wither from lack of sunlight.'

Annie fidgeted. 'I'm going to head out.'

'Are you ready for another challenge?' I asked.

The resoundingly enthusiastic yes made me feel remiss, like a school teacher with students complaining about lack of homework.

'It might be harder than it sounds. I know that you love Rome, but I want you to go out and search for at least five things you can't stand about it.'

Annie looked puzzled. 'What do you mean? Buildings I hate? Or tourist attractions?'

'Anything. Places, habits, people, food.'

'That might be a tall order for one day,' Annie said, already twitching to shoot off.

'I'm not expecting you to do it all straightaway. Take as long as you need, a couple of days, or a week.' The whole point of the tasks we set was to push our guests out of their comfort zones so they continuously had to question themselves, rather than discovering an easy answer in a few hours.

Annie was already running down the steps, her surfer's hair bobbing up and down. I often felt that our conversations were unfinished, that just when I had a sense of what she needed, she darted out of reach, a torn leaflet of wisdom whirling away in her slipstream.

I peered along the corridor to Nadia's apartment. I should let her come to me when she was ready. I hadn't seen her go out for any food, though. Taking a fresh pineapple out of the fridge, I chopped bite-sized pieces into a bowl, then added in some watermelon. I thought about nuts but wasn't sure if pregnant women were allowed to eat them any more and didn't want to mark myself out as a grandmother that couldn't be trusted even before the birth.

I carried over a tray and rapped on the door. Nadia took ages to open it. Her demeanour had all the welcome of a horse chestnut fruit. I ploughed on. 'I wondered if you wanted something to eat.' She didn't step aside. Nerves made me state the obvious. 'Pineapple and watermelon. You like fruit,' I said as though she was a suspicious toddler that I was trying to win round. 'It's good for the baby.'

As soon as the words were out of my mouth, I wanted to suck them back in.

Nadia sighed but took the tray from me. 'Thank you.'

I breathed out. 'How are you feeling?'

'Fat. Discombobulated. Hot. Being pregnant in the summer has to be the worst.'

Discombobulated. I'd forgotten that word even existed. I didn't comment, didn't think right now was the moment for a trip down linguistic lane. 'You'll forget about all of this when the baby's born.'

I had expected Nadia to invite me into my own apartment but it seemed I'd be in for a long wait.

'Are you getting everything sorted? Do you need a hand with anything?'

'No. I'm all good.'

I managed to trap my observation about whether it was normal in England to say 'I'm good' rather than 'I'm well' or 'I'm fine' before it hit the atmosphere.

'Right, you know where I am if you need me. Would you like to come to dinner with Annie and Marina the day after tomorrow?' I asked. Ridiculous that I needed to give her two days' notice to prepare herself to sit opposite me with a plate of pasta. Conversing with the mother of my first and probably only grandchild was giving me an insight into how stand-up comedians felt in tough working men's clubs.

'Can I let you know later?' she asked.

'Of course,' I said, conjuring up a smile so big my cheeks burst into my peripheral vision. I'd keep my attention on the big prize.

In the end, everyone came for dinner. I hadn't spelt out to Nadia the fact that Marina and I were setting up challenges for the tenants who came to live here. Inevitably, Annie started talking about what I'd asked her to do in the latest one, which, of course, she'd completed in record time.

Nadia put her hand up. 'Sorry to interrupt, Annie. My mum and Marina have got you running around doing some weird Anglo-Italian reality show set in Rome?' I wasn't sure she could have sounded any more derogatory, but Annie was unfazed.

'I love it. It's a great way to see Rome through a different lens. And because I'm on my own, I'm really looking, properly taking notice of everything. If I was with someone, I'd be nattering away about any old drivel and missing out on so many details.' Annie grinned. 'You're so lucky to have grown up here. Being bilingual is such an amazing gift.'

Nadia had the grace to agree. 'I probably take it for granted because it's normal for me.'

'Presumably you'll speak English to the baby?'

Nadia wound her mushroom tagliatelle around her fork. 'I haven't decided yet.'

She was like a skunk sending out warning puffs of pong that no one should presume anything about her choices.

Annie glanced around as though she expected me to back her up. There was a woman who hadn't yet understood that snipers could be hiding in every sentence, and if she wanted to avoid getting caught in the crossfire, she needed to tuck herself into the shelter of silence.

Marina did understand but was quite happy to stroll brazenly out into the open without so much as a flak jacket. 'Ronnie can teach your baby English if you'd rather speak Italian.'

My smile was becoming more strained. 'Nadia will no doubt work out what's best over time,' I said, relaxing as my daughter changed the subject.

'So what's the point of this challenge? What did you say it was, Annie? Five awful things about Rome?' She frowned at me. 'Why are you getting her to look at the negatives?'

I had no choice but to put my reasoning out there. 'I've been thinking a lot recently about how we can choose to emphasise the negatives in the world, tell ourselves everything is terrible and drag ourselves down.' I ignored Nadia's accusatory glare and concentrated on the conviction that had prompted the idea in the first place. 'But, really, life is more nuanced than that. As far as I can see, Annie loves Rome, which is brilliant. However, it's always good to recognise the imperfections and make a conscious decision to focus on the positives, rather than pretending they don't exist.'

Marina laughed out loud. 'That's genius. We could do that for people as well. We could all list each other's flaws, then decide whether the good traits outweigh the bad. Shall I begin with you, Ron?'

I put my hand up. 'No. We are absolutely not doing that.'

Marina topped up her wineglass. 'Spoilsport. *Vigliacca.*'

A coward, yes, but not stupid. I didn't want to furnish Nadia with any more ammunition about my inadequacies than she had amassed already.

'So, Annie, have you come across anything you don't like in Rome?' I asked.

'It feels a bit churlish to turn up here and start pointing out things I don't like, a bit Little Englander with a superiority complex.'

'I specifically asked you to do it. No one will be offended.'

'It depends what she says,' Marina said, unhelpfully.

Nadia snorted. 'You got offended when you were offered a seat on a bus, so we're going to discount your view on what's insulting.'

Marina waggled her forefinger. 'The woman was older than me! I'm not yet at the stage where someone who's got one foot in the grave needs to haul her old skeleton up so I can sit down.'

Annie surprised me. She giggled, then did that thing I recognised so well. She tried to smother her mirth on the grounds that over-laughing might be a bit rude but drew more attention to herself by bursting out with a loud splutter and chuckling helplessly. It was so long since I'd laughed like that, though I remembered it as a prominent feature of Sunday mornings in church when I was a child. It was an affliction that had persisted into adulthood, rearing its head at the most inopportune moments. I'd trained myself out of it in my early twenties, when I'd met Eddie. He was not a man you could laugh at. But in the candlelight, with the earthy smell of porcini mushrooms and the tang of parmesan filling the air, her hilarity infected us all and even Marina rode the wave, saying, 'What next? A hearse will stop for me and say, "Want a lift? We're going your way. Save you a bus fare."'

I glanced at my daughter, her face lit up with uncomplicated fun. She looked younger, the ghost of that little girl begging to see the Christmas tree and life-size nativity scene in St Peter's Square. We'd always told her that the Pope had created the tradition especially for her in 1982, to celebrate her first birthday. Every year when she was old enough, we'd make a game out of guessing which European country would provide the tree. We'd carried on the ritual until Matteo died. He was the self-proclaimed champion after his long-shot guess of

Romania in 2001. Our life together wasn't all bad. And tonight was as good as it had been for a long time. We might even have passed for a normal family.

Eventually, we all calmed down from imagining increasingly dramatic scenarios to offend Marina and let Annie take the floor. She flicked through her photos. 'So, firstly, what's with all the rubbish? The heat makes it smell so rancid.'

A rat had run over Marina's foot when she was eating at one of her favourite restaurants, so we were all willing to accept that was a downside to the city. 'It's always been a bit of an issue, but since a landfill site was closed several years ago, it's got worse. Though the upside for you is that when you're back in England, you'll never moan that your bin has been missed after a bank holiday. What else?'

'Do drivers in Rome get points for mowing people down on pedestrian crossings? Half the time, they seem to accelerate. Are there national statistics for road traffic accidents when tourists thought they were safe to cross?'

Nadia laughed. 'There's an ageist, sexist system to it. If you're a woman under the age of twenty-five, most men will slow down. If you're over seventy with a stick, they probably will as well. Everyone else in between, look out.'

Annie glanced around the table. 'But don't the police issue fines? I'm such a scaredy-cat, my sons laugh at me because I stop at crossings when people would have to break a world speed record to step in front of me.'

Marina flicked her hand at Annie in the way she did at me when I became too English. 'Enough, enough with all the rules. That rush of adrenaline every time you navigate a road reminds you you're alive. Next!'

Annie said, 'I'd never have come up with that as a positive, but, yes, there's a certain dangerous appeal to that.' She peered at her list. 'This is another traffic-related one. What's with the parking in the middle of roundabouts or on the keep-clear chevrons? Surely you get a ticket for that.'

I left it to Marina to share her logic on this one. 'I can't see the problem. After a certain age, you should be able to leave the car close to wherever you're going. And if the government don't make enough convenient spaces, then you have to be inventive.' She folded her hands into her lap. 'Besides, it was never a difficulty for me. I have friends very high up in the traffic police.'

'But if everyone parks anywhere they want, doesn't it lead to chaos?' Annie asked.

'It will only be a certain sector of the population,' I said. 'I'm always pretty law-abiding, because I don't want the aggro of being towed away, whereas Marina, when she was still driving, didn't care.'

'We shouldn't go through life blindly following rules without asking ourselves if they're necessary,' Marina said.

Nadia nudged Marina. 'You never think any rule is necessary unless it's one you've invented yourself.'

'Precisely,' Marina replied, as though Nadia had sided with her and proved her point.

I turned to Annie. 'So the upside to everyone abandoning their cars wherever they want is that apparently it shows a healthy disrespect for authority.'

'As well as imagination, initiative, and an ability to problem-solve,' Marina added.

Nadia's face took on the serious expression that preceded a lecture. 'The simple solution is to take a bus or the metro and stop polluting into the bargain.'

I moved the conversation on before we all floundered under melting ice caps and plastic particles in our waterways. 'So what else gives you a realistic impression of Rome?'

'It's ironic that I'm coming up with this, but don't the people who live here get sick to death of tourists? Yesterday, I was out and about when everyone was walking to work and there were all these people in shorts blocking the pavements, stopping suddenly to take photos.'

I tried to tread a middle path. 'Summer is particularly bad, but don't forget a lot of Romans disappear off to the seaside or mountains in July or August, so then it's mainly tourists annoying other tourists. It's a double-edged sword really. There are about ten million visitors a year, so they bring a lot of money to the city. Think of all the restaurants, hotels, tour guides, taxis, buskers that rely on tourism to survive.'

'I suppose so. I guess it depends on your perspective, but I'd hate to work near the Trevi Fountain and greet every day with a selfie stick jammed in my ear.'

I clapped my hands. 'That's why I chose this challenge. Perspective. That for every negative, every thing that annoys us, there is often a positive if we look hard enough.'

Marina tapped her walking stick on the terracotta tiles in case there was any chance we were going to ignore her. 'Has the sun fried your tiny mind? What's the positive about wasps? Or dog poo? Or pigeons?' She emptied the last of the red wine into her glass. 'I rest my case.'

Marina's argumentative nature always increased in direct correlation to her alcohol consumption.

I sighed. 'You're being obstreperous,' I said, delighting in a word I rarely got to use. I occasionally caught Marina out by choosing obscure terms she hadn't learnt from her Irish dad. Not this time, though.

'I'm not. You're making ridiculous claims that you can't back up.'

'I don't want to get into the whole usefulness or otherwise of wildlife and their waste products. I just thought it was a good exercise for Annie, to see if she could think about some of the things that have caused issues in her family in a different way.'

Nadia leaned forward on her elbow. 'So does that mean you're suddenly going to appreciate my ability to keep secrets?'

The cold fear of confrontation jolted me from that cosy sense of diverse women together, different ages, exchanging wide-ranging life experiences and having a bit of light-hearted fun. I tried to laugh it off. 'I've always appreciated your many talents, darling.'

Nadia wavered. I saw it on her face. The battle between letting the good times roll and the surge of resentment, of bitterness, that my words had ignited.

Fiery and feisty won out. 'It's the hypocrisy that kills me. You've absolutely focused on the negative, blaming me for not telling you that Dad was being unfaithful. You could have chosen to see that I did what I thought was best. I hoped it would come to a natural conclusion without you ever having to know. I was trying to stop you getting hurt, not add to it.'

I glanced at Annie, who was staring into her lap, her eyes flicking up now and again, as though she was gauging how she could make a bolt for the door without anyone noticing.

I stood up and started clearing the plates. 'Nadia, shall we discuss that another time?'

'You chose to invite total strangers to live here instead of Grant and me when I asked you back in December. So I'm assuming you consider them more part of the family than I am, which means we don't have to creep about pretending we're the Waltons.' She turned to Annie and said, 'No offence, I'm sure you're very nice.'

Annie surprised me. 'I'm probably like most people. A mixture of nice and downright difficult. I'm not sure what has gone on between you and it's none of my business either, but I will just say that I would have loved a mum like yours. Believe me, you've been very lucky. My impression is that she would do anything for you, especially now there's a baby on the way.'

Marina was looking from one to the other as though she was watching an entertaining match between two tennis players with different strengths. She appeared no more anxious than if she was dispassionately assessing whether the twisty backhand would triumph over the sneaky top-spin serve.

Nadia didn't show a flicker of sympathy for Annie, whose mother – if she was worse than me – was the absolute pits. 'Yeah, that's precisely it. Now she knows I'm expecting her first grandchild, she's all excited grandma-in-waiting. But rewind back a few months, some other woman – Beth, was it? – was far more important, someone she had no connection with simply had to have the apartment. I was pregnant, for goodness' sake! I thought I might be able to persuade Grant to move out to Rome, where everything is so much more family-friendly, so he'd see that we'd still have a life.'

I hadn't known Nadia was pregnant then, yet guilt still rushed through me at how I'd connived with Marina to keep my daughter away. I was tempted to hit back that maybe if she'd have communicated, I might have seen things differently. However, reasoning with Nadia when she had her dander up like this was impossible.

I picked up the crockery and carried it into the kitchen, afraid to respond because I couldn't guarantee my reaction. I might have pinpointed all the things I had got right, the millions of caring actions she'd either been totally oblivious to or not appreciated enough. Or I'd have burst into tears and done an over-the-top apology for my myriad failures as a mother. Neither approach would have swayed Nadia. She always fought anger with her own brand of red-hot fury, but she'd never been a fan of chest-beating mea culpa either. In that, she reminded me of Matteo. It had never been easy to apologise to him. He'd simply say, 'I'm not interested in you being sorry. I'm interested in it not happening again.' Nadia had that same hard edge.

Marina's voice, however, carried on the night air, oddly conciliatory for someone who was only in favour of drama if she starred in the leading role. 'Nadia, *cara. Amore.*' I was half-expecting her kind tone to be a sheep in wolf's clothing that would suddenly bare its teeth and segue into her illogical belief that a period of harsh national service was the antidote to people bemoaning their lot. She switched into Italian as she always did when she wanted to speak from the heart. I was surprised to hear her explaining that it had taken a long time for me to process Matteo's betrayal. She added that it was unfortunate that Nadia had known about the affair and I had not (true), that Nadia hadn't clearly explained her motive for wanting to come to Rome for an extended period (true) and that, anyway, by the time I'd received her letter, we'd already promised the flat to Beth (false). I loved Marina for lying for me, though if I thanked her, she'd say, 'Recollections may vary,' channelling her inner Queen Elizabeth and doubling the corgis.

Nadia wasn't rolling over. She couldn't understand why we wanted strangers in the palazzo in the first place, at which point, I heard Annie say softly, 'I think I'll leave you to it. Goodnight.'

When she came into the kitchen, I scraped together the last vestiges of stoicism to apologise for our mother-daughter dynamics hijacking the focus from her own. I was expecting her to rush for the door, but she marched straight over and caught me off guard by enveloping me in a big hug.

'Thank you. You're amazing, and I meant what I said, I wish my mother had been like you.'

I shook my head. 'I made so many mistakes.'

Annie looked me straight in the eye. 'What parent doesn't? How do any of us know what the right thing to do is? With my two boys, the right thing for one could be entirely the wrong thing for the other. My eldest, Dylan, was a shocker when he was a teenager, quite out of control, even before I divorced my husband, but especially afterwards.'

'How do you mean?' I asked, somewhat half-heartedly as I

was straining to overhear how effectively Marina was fighting my corner.

Annie sighed as though the list of Dylan's misdemeanours was endless. 'He could never foresee the consequences of his actions and because he never spoke to me about anything, I had no way of talking him out of all the risky and sometimes down-right dangerous schemes he dreamed up. I spent my life hanging around in the kitchen so that when he came home, I could harvest clues about what he was up to.' She laughed. 'I was a bit like a fisherman casting a hook into an underpopulated river. I basically learnt what was happening when I was called into school every time he got close to being expelled.'

There was something intrinsically kind about Annie, her willingness to share her own difficulties, but a teenage boy not confiding in his mother couldn't compete with the arctic wind howling through my relationship with Nadia.

She glanced towards the terrace, where Nadia was weaving between her two mother tongues, strangely logical in Italian and fierce and emotional in English. 'I've never felt Mum was very interested in me. So far, at different times, I've lived in England for ten years – four at uni, and the last six – and she's barely bothered to visit. She's always relied on me coming home.'

I pretended I couldn't hear and busied myself tucking the prosciutto into the wax paper and putting it back in the fridge, throwing a little bit of fat to Strega as a reward for never criti-cising my dog-parenting abilities.

Annie touched my arm. 'I'm going to bed now. Thank you for dinner.'

On impulse, I swung round. 'I don't believe your mother didn't love you. She must have done. You don't have the spiky edges of someone who wasn't loved enough.'

Annie shrugged. 'Maybe she just didn't show it in the way I wanted. I had a kind of godmother who really believed in me, so perhaps that balanced her out.'

At my age, it was rare that I met someone whose company I actively pursued. Since Matteo had died, some of the people I'd considered joint friends had turned out to be solely my husband's. My double whammy of widowhood and long-term betrayed spouse acted like a reverse magnet. Others I'd weeded out because of my reduced tolerance for anyone who did too much head-tilting. I'd also culled those who appeared more mesmerised by the gritty detail of Matteo's behaviour than how I was faring. I'd had a camera installed so I could ignore whoever was at the door when it suited me.

Annie was different. Her enthusiasm for life was contagious.

'Would you come with me tomorrow? There's another challenge that I think would be good for both of us,' I said.

Her face lit up. 'I'd love to.'

'Nine o'clock, before it gets too hot.'

'What's the point of this one?' Annie asked.

'I'll let you work that out,' I said at exactly the same moment as Nadia's words, 'I should never have come back,' filtered through to the kitchen.

12

As soon as Annie had left, I'd gone out onto the terrace and said to Nadia, 'I'm sorry. None of this was your fault. I wish you hadn't been caught in the middle. It was awful that your dad put you in a position of having to keep a secret for all those years.'

Nadia pushed her chair back. 'See, you say you're sorry, but then you shove all the blame onto Dad. You have to accept some responsibility too.'

I'd expected my apology to defuse the situation rather than stoke it up, so I was slow to respond to the counterattack.

Nadia was spoiling for a fight, though. 'You haven't got an answer to that, have you? It's so much easier to be the innocent victim than to acknowledge that there's a problem and try to fix it.'

I could feel the flame of the wine I'd consumed playing chicken with a tinderbox of things I shouldn't say out loud. Hallelujah for being old enough to know that late-night mud-slinging never ended with the other person calming down and accepting that they were out of order. I took a second to find the right tone of voice, glaring at Marina to keep her tuppence-worth to herself. She puffed her cheeks out as though the words she wanted to say were battling for an exit. I tapped into every last scrap of wisdom I'd amassed over seventy-four years about not needing to win an argument. Through gritted teeth, I managed, 'You've probably got a point. Can I say, though, that I'm really glad you came back? That I hope you'll stay?'

These were the right words to deliver in that moment, but I wasn't sure whether I fully believed them. I longed to have total faith in what I'd said. I wanted to be that magnanimous mother, but I had a sneaking suspicion I was slyly angling for the moral high ground. That when challenged later, I could roll this conversation out as proof that I'd held my hands up to my poor behaviour, shown myself to be forgiving and nothing but supportive to Nadia. That wasn't really a topic covered in *The Common Sense Book of Baby and Child Care* my mother had sent me when Nadia was born. As far as I could remember, the bet-hedging conversations to get you out of Dodge with your adult children was an epilogue yet to be written.

However, it was sufficient for Nadia to say, with slightly less hostility, 'Thank you.' And then, rather ungratefully, 'I can't go anywhere until after the baby is born anyway.'

I forbade my tender heart to entertain the threat of Nadia hopping onto a plane with my grandchild in an ethically sourced sling, encouraged to wave at me on our weekly Face-Time slots but never to know the grandmotherly love I intended to embed deep into his psyche.

In an uncharacteristically diplomatic manoeuvre, Marina came to my rescue by deciding that we all needed a good sleep and shuffled Nadia off. Her words, 'Ronnie loves you. She'll be a godsend when the baby's born' echoed along the hallway. I was too exhausted to brace myself for Nadia's reply and shut the door.

. . .

I'd been up for ages by the time Annie joined me in the courtyard the next morning. Sleep had eluded me, my mind preferring instead to replay the dying embers of last night's grudge barbecue. My heart felt heavy, the bruise of my relationship with Nadia making my body ache and sag.

Annie blew in all perky and expectant by way of contrast. She was in tight white cut-off jeans and a T-shirt, her shaggy haircut giving her the appearance of a blonde Suzi Quatro, all feisty moves and attitude. 'Devil Gate Drive' came into my head, the lyrics as clear and bold as when I first heard them on the radio. Number one during the February half-term of 1974. Forty-nine years ago, when I couldn't imagine being old. When I still believed in a happy-ever-after with Eddie. When I thought love was enough, and everything – *everything* – else was peripheral.

I recoiled from the memory and started the Vespa, Strega barking indignantly on the terrace as she heard the exhaust rattle. I nodded to Annie. 'Hop on behind me.'

We sped off, the warm air of the morning flapping my harem pants like a pair of purple wings. My spirits lifted as I heard the little gasps and squeaks behind me while I manoeuvred my way through the traffic. I looped around the Vatican and parked down a side street.

Annie handed me her helmet. 'You are so cool. My mother would never have had the courage to roar about on a motorbike in a city like this. You're like Audrey Hepburn in *Roman Holiday* – but a better driver.'

I was too battered to take any pleasure in the flattering comparison with Audrey Hepburn, let alone another mother, who, truth be known, had probably done her best. 'I moved to Rome just before I was thirty. I learnt to ride the Vespa when I still thought I was invincible.' I let the lie skitter away across the pavement; I had already known then that no one was invincible. I set off in the direction of St Peter's Square. 'I know you've already been here, but I wanted to show you something you might have missed.'

I led her to a marble circle between the obelisk in the centre of the square and the fountain to my left.

'If you stand here, and look at the nearest colonnade, you'll see that, from this point, Bernini designed all the columns to line up so that you can only see a single row around the square, and not the rows behind.'

Annie took my spot, trying out my theory, squinting, stepping to the left and right. 'There's not much of a margin for error. It's hard to believe they could be so exact in the seventeenth century without the benefit of technology. That's so clever. I'd never have noticed that.'

I flicked up my forefinger. 'Hold that thought while I take you somewhere else.'

There was something refreshing about observing Rome through Annie's eyes. Marina kept moaning that she'd come out here on false pretences – 'I've seen a snoozing kitten more troubled than she is.' I had to agree that she didn't seem too distressed about her mother and my attempts to ask if she'd had contact with her sister were brushed away – 'I expect she'll get in touch when she wants me to help her clear out my mum's kitchen. It'll be handbags at dawn over the Teasmade.' Frankly, though, I was glad that she wasn't sitting in a shattered heap. I loved her curiosity about Rome. And I adored the optimistic slant to her nature, such a valuable shield against circumstance. Guiltily, I found her so much easier to be around than Nadia, and it was refreshing to have someone other than Strega always eager for my company.

Fifteen minutes later, I pulled up near Galleria Spada. We entered into the palatial building and I led her through to the garden courtyard. We stood looking down a long corridor, enclosed by ornate arches and pillars. It was the sort of romantic pergola where star-crossed lovers in breeches and long skirts run towards each other for their happy-ever-after. At the end, there was a statue of Mars.

'How long do you think this walkway is?' I asked.

Annie grimaced. 'I'm no good at measuring distance. Twenty metres? Thirty?'

'What about the statue? How high do you think it is?'

She hesitated, afraid of disappointing me. 'I don't know. Two metres?'

'Wait there.'

I peered round to check there was no one about and stepped over the little chain barrier designed to stop the public doing what I was about to do. I hurried towards the statue, knowing that the height of the pillars would be shrinking around me until I reached the figure of Mars and towered over it.

When I turned back, Annie's mouth was open in an expression of delight and surprise. 'How does that even happen?'

'The cardinal who owned the building, Spada, wanted a big garden, but there wasn't enough room because it's slap bang in the city centre. So he got Borromini to design an optical illusion. Look, the ground slopes upwards, the ceiling drops, the columns are much smaller and the corridor is narrower at the far end to give the illusion of length and height. The walkway is only about ten metres long.'

'That's incredible. From a distance, I thought that statue was taller than me. I could fit it into my handbag!'

'It's actually eighty centimetres high.'

'I love this.' Annie rubbed her face on her sleeve. 'But I'm baking hot already. Can I buy you a coffee or water somewhere?'

'Are you sure you don't want to see the paintings inside? There's a Titian and a Gentileschi?' I didn't want her to miss out but ditching the art for a drink in the shade was very tempting.

She gestured towards the exit. 'I'll come back another day.'

'Okay, let's go and find a café.' I shot my finger into the air as another idea occurred to me. 'If we go via Palazzo Farnese to Piazza Campo de' Fiori, I'll buy Nadia some flowers from the market as a peace offering.'

As we left Galleria Spada, Annie said, 'Is peace a possibility?' – a question I thought was brave but probably reflected her own uncertainty about her relationship with her sister.

'I have to believe it is. She was always much closer to her dad, but I'm holding onto hope that motherhood might soften her. Perhaps she'll become more forgiving of my faults when she sees that bringing up children can be a bit hit-and-miss.'

We stepped into the road to avoid being flattened by a Segway tour.

Annie tutted. 'I stand by what I said about other tourists annoying me.'

'It's funny, isn't it, how when you are somewhere for a decent stretch of time, you start to feel superior to anyone who's just there for a long weekend?' I laughed.

We turned in to Piazza Farnese. I showed her the French embassy, where a part of its façade sported a huge piece of 3D artwork. It gave the impression of splitting open the building itself and exposing the statues, ornate cornices and panelling of the interior.

'Yet another *trompe l'oeil*. This one is brilliant, because it's covering the renovation work behind it. It's done by a French street artist called JR.' I pointed. 'See that statue of Hercules? The real one is in a museum in Naples, but it was part of the palazzo's original collection. I like the idea that he's put it back there temporarily.'

Annie was fascinated. 'Oh my goodness. That must have taken so much planning. Only a city like Rome could have managed to turn scaffolding into a thing of beauty. If that was London, we'd all be looking at grey plastic sheets for two years.'

I squeezed her arm. 'Don't fall into the trap of thinking that the grass is always greener here. England has so much to recommend it as well.'

Annie raised her eyebrows. 'Says the woman who avoids going back at all costs.'

I flicked my hand out in a gesture of defeat but didn't offer any explanation.

We took the two seats left in partial shade at the café nearest to the flower stalls, where I'd chosen a bunch of white gladioli for Nadia. I was tempted to buy a peace lily in a pot but wasn't sure she'd appreciate the humour. I ordered a Crodino – 'It's like a Campari without the alcohol' – and a cappuccino for Annie. 'Italians are very snobby about people drinking cappuccino after eleven. It's almost like it's in their genes to reject that as a concept. I think you have to grow up here to care. A bit like swearing in Italian. I recognise that the words are rude, but I don't have the same visceral reaction as when I hear them in English.'

Annie grinned. 'It's quite tempting to let loose a string of obscenities and test your theory when you say that.'

I didn't want Annie to think I was a total fuddy-duddy, so I said, 'I'm not averse to the odd eff and blind myself, but the way I hear people swear on TV, especially the British programmes, is quite horrible. Even the C-word doesn't seem to be a taboo now. I don't think I'd heard anyone say it in front of me until I was in my twenties.' I shuddered as I remembered the first time I'd heard it aimed at me.

When our drinks arrived, Annie said, 'So, should I hazard a guess about the purpose of today's challenge?'

I took a sip. 'Go on, then.'

'Were you trying to emphasise that there are unexpected things everywhere if we open our eyes?'

I wrinkled my nose. 'Sort of. A bit more specific.'

'That what we see depends on where we focus our attention?'

'Yes, that's about right. It's really about perspective again. We all have a tendency to think we've got the monopoly on the truth of any given situation. But I can't help feeling that if we just move our minds slightly to the left or right, a bit like in St Peter's Square, you have an entirely different panorama.'

Annie wiped at her froth moustache. 'How did you even come up with that?'

I never got the impression that Annie was judging me. I was more open with her than most people I'd known for a lifetime. 'Since Matteo died, I've had more opportunities than I could have wished for to see things from a different stance. When Matteo's mistress turned up at the hospice and then again for his funeral, I was absolutely livid. Raging. But from her standpoint, she'd loved him for decades and wanted to pay her respects.'

Annie looked horrified. 'So is what she wanted more important than the fallout – causing you embarrassment, putting Nadia in a difficult position, effectively compounding the hurt she'd already caused?'

'That's where perspective comes in.' I laughed. 'For what it's worth, I still think she's a conniving witch. But I could elect to see it differently. If you take the Vatican, for example, you can stand where we were and see one row of columns or adjust your position and see several. Both perspectives are still beautiful. In the case of Borromini's corridor, from one point of view, it's genius. Close up, however, it's a bit disappointing, akin to understanding the mechanics behind a brilliant magic trick. We can choose to admire it, or obsess about how he swindled us into thinking it's a much bigger space.'

Annie stirred her coffee, licking the teaspoon. 'Am I right in assuming that you'd like me to carry this idea over into my approach with my mother and my sister?'

'That's for you to decide. What I will say is that knowing Matteo had been unfaithful to me for years skewed my recollection of our whole history together. In many ways, I feel as though I lived a lie, but there were still some parts that were real. And good. We were a great team. And if it wasn't for Matteo, I would have had a much more difficult life in Italy.'

'How do you mean?' Annie asked.

'To begin with, he was Italian, so he knew how everything worked, how to make things happen. Back in the eighties, everything – getting a job, even finding a flat wasn't straightforward unless you were *raccomandato*. Everything was easier if you knew someone, if you had an uncle or a father or a godparent who worked in the right place, or a friend who owed you a favour. It was through a friend of Matteo's, who had connections with multinational food businesses, that I managed to make a career out of translating.'

Annie pulled a face. 'Like an old boys' network?'

'Yes, but more acceptable somehow. People were quite open about it. I suppose if I hadn't met Matteo, I might have ended up skulking back to England with my tail between my legs.' I pushed away the familiar stab of regret that I hadn't made any attempt to reconcile with my parents before it was too late.

'Was it a whirlwind romance?'

I leaned back in my chair. 'Not really, though we got married quite quickly. By the time I met Matteo, I'd already had the fairy-tale love affair that hadn't been a fairy tale at all – quite the opposite. I didn't want to be that out of control again. I was more transactional, I suppose. More practical. And I'm not sure I admitted this, but the clock was ticking. By the time I had Nadia, at thirty-three, I was two years off being classed as a geriatric mother! The cheek of it. I don't consider myself geriatric now.'

Annie sniffed. 'I don't know how anyone who zips about on a Vespa could be considered geriatric.'

I paused, reflecting that I could never regret my relationship with him because he'd given me Nadia. Alongside the bitterness I'd felt towards him over the last few years, there was something softer there too, gratitude perhaps. As well as a reluctant recognition that he'd appeared in my world at a time when I was directionless and lonely. I could never have admitted to Nadia – whom I'd brought up to be fiercely independent – what it was that had propelled me into her father's arms. In fact, I'd taken ages to acknowledge it myself: after the turmoil of the preceding years in England, it had been a relief to make a clean break with the past and hitch myself to someone uncomplicated, who already had life sorted. Matteo was an architect, with his own practice and an apartment in Villa Alba. In the beginning, at least, he'd been drawn to the fact that I was foreign, a bit unconventional. He'd loved showing off his city with the pride of a true *romano*. It had been so easy to be swept along into his slipstream.

Annie put her hand over mine. 'Do you mind talking about this? We've had such a lovely morning. I don't want to make you sad.'

'I don't mind at all. It's quite reassuring to say it out loud and not feel I might double over with the hurt of it all. But I don't want to bore you.'

'I have never found you boring. Ever.'

How had Annie's mother not treasured her? Maybe there was an argument for setting up a website that matched misunderstood mothers with other people's adult daughters – 'Vespa-riding, dog-loving mother, partial to a bit of tie-dye, can cook a comforting lasagne and sit up late drinking wine in times of both crisis and celebration. Seeks daughter that she doesn't always have to second-guess and with whom eggshells are not required.'

I suggested it to Annie, whose face crinkled up with mischief. 'I reckon it could go down a storm. All these daughters who think other people's parents are fabulous but have spent their lives with their stomachs clenching at their mother's suggestion that they need a coat or an umbrella or that they might look a bit smarter with a "dab of lipstick".' She nudged me. 'Perhaps we could set up Tinder for mothers and daughters.'

I didn't miss the quizzical glance in my direction. 'I'm not so ancient and out of touch that I don't know what Tinder is. Are you on it?'

Annie looked mortified. 'Absolutely not. I'd probably end up stumbling across my sons' friends that they were at primary school with.' She guided me back to our earlier conversation. 'Anyway, you were saying you'd started to appreciate the good things about your husband despite his affair.'

'Oh yes. Crikey, perhaps this is the first sign of senility, not being able to stay on topic.'

Annie wagged her finger at me. 'From my *perspective*, it's the sign of an intelligent brain with many wise words clamouring to get out.'

'Pah, I love your delusion. Anyway, I'd better carry on before I wander off on another tangent. It was very complicated initially, because there was the straightforward grief at Matteo's death – if grief can ever be considered straightforward – and the complex grief around discovering that our marriage wasn't what I thought. So those two things were running side by side. But, weirdly, knowing that he'd loved someone else as well as me, or maybe instead of me – although I think it was more likely he couldn't choose between us – was also quite liberating. There didn't seem so much point in tethering myself to the past, because it wasn't the anchor I thought it was. Not quite the same necessity to wear my widowhood with such prominence.' I finished my drink. 'Sorry, I'm wittering on. And there you were, looking forward to a jolly jaunt around some hidden treasures in Rome.'

I ordered some water and poured us each a glass.

'I can feel my fingers swelling in the heat. I've never managed to drink as much liquid as I should. Nadia is always telling me off.' I suddenly felt self-conscious, as though I was slotting straight into the cliché of an old woman rambling on. 'Anyway, how are you feeling about everything? Are you finding any answers in these old stones of Rome?'

'Me? I'm fine, thank you. Not sure what answers I expected to find.'

I felt tired. Too tired to prise open the sardine can of Annie with an uncooperative key. Maybe she was the one with the real perspective in all of this. Her mother preferred her sister, she was now dead so there was nothing she could do to change that, so she'd decided not to let it blight her joy moving forwards. I was sure, however, that sort of reasoning didn't happen overnight, especially when combined with the implosion of her relationship with her sister, whom she 'adored'.

Ridiculously, irrationally, unfairly, I felt irritated with Annie for not speaking to her sister and telling her that it didn't matter what either of them thought about their parents' marriage, it didn't matter that each other's versions of their childhood were north and south. Annie was still young; she could have thirty or forty years of good times with her sister. She didn't need to be right. She just had to accept that in every family there are fifty-five versions of the truth. That everyone trimmed the facts to show themselves in a superior light, tailoring the past to something they could bear to live with.

'So when are you going to contact your sister?' I said, hearing an overbearing note creep into my voice. I felt perilously close to throwing a tantrum. All these people bringing hammer blows down on the connections they should cherish the most. Arguments about stuff that couldn't be changed, that existed in the nebulous haze of family history, where no one person was right. Me included.

She took a long slug of water but didn't duck the question. Quite the opposite. She stared straight at me. 'I'll get in touch when I've figured out something I've wanted to understand for years.'

And before I could dig any further, she disappeared to the loo and the moment rolled away, like a marble under a sofa.

13

Over the next week, Nadia seemed calmer, as though letting off
steam had burst the pustule of resentment. I even dared to
suggest we take a taxi to the Chicco baby store to get a few
essentials. I tried not to transmit my panic that the baby was due
in less than three weeks. As far as I could see, Nadia didn't
possess a single nappy, let alone a cot. I couldn't marry this up
with the woman who decanted everything into glass jars and
was fastidious about recycling every last scrap of paper but was
leaving a huge life event to chance. She'd shot me down in
flames when I'd asked her what arrangements she'd made for
the birth, which hospital she was in contact with. 'It's all under
control. I sorted it all out before I left England.'

Nadia would have made a brilliant enforcer of 'careless talk
costs lives' propaganda in the Second World War.

I'd nearly choked on the sarcasm I'd had to swallow when
I'd stated in the most neutral tone I could muster, 'I know you're
very capable, but in case things move quickly, you'd better tell
me where you need to go.'

'I'm having the baby here. There's a midwife coming to the
house. I'm having a water birth.'

I'd squashed down the 'What happens if she doesn't get here in time? Marina is useless in a medical crisis and my midwifery experience is limited to yanking a calf out by its feet about sixty years ago'. I opted instead for: 'Great. Should I have her number just in case?'

Nadia wanted to resist, but there was a flicker of fear, of vulnerability. Her desire to reiterate that she didn't need anyone, least of all me, finally gave in to common sense. I sagged with relief. I wished Nadia had had her baby ten years ago when I was a bit younger and could have run for help at speed.

Marina proved herself to be a great ally and became far more no-nonsense about Nadia's lack of preparation than I would ever have dared. 'I've organised Federico to drive us over to Chicco tomorrow. Otherwise at this rate you're going to be putting that baby to sleep in a drawer.'

I glared at Marina. That would be the ultimate upcycling project to appeal to Nadia's eco-motivation. I could quite envisage a scenario in which the baby would be nestling down on a straw-stuffed pillowcase in the bottom of a wardrobe.

Thankfully, Nadia didn't latch onto the suggestion and she simply asked, 'Who's Federico?'

Marina stuck out her hip provocatively. 'Just one of my many admirers. His son renovated these apartments. He'd do *anything* for me.' It was one of our most bonding moments to date as Nadia and I rolled our eyes in unison.

'How old is he?'

Marina said, 'Oh, young. Early seventies. He can be our packhorse.'

'He's not going to trail round a baby shop with us, though, is he?'

'Oh no. I'm not either. Federico and I will go and drink cocktails or something. I'm a bit allergic to all that fecundity bouncing about like bumper cars.'

'Would you like me to come with you?' I asked, filling Nadia's hesitation with 'I don't mind either way.'

'No, I think I'll be better off on my own. Each generation has such a different view on what newborns need.'

I sucked back down the words I wanted to say as though inhaling menthol vapour during a cold: 'Love, food, warmth and security are pretty universal.' Instead, I focused on my goal: proving to Nadia that I could be an excellent grandma and it would be madness to move back to England to a man who didn't want her. I chose not to dwell on how recently I'd been concocting a scheme to prevent Nadia residing in the same building as me. It was my comeuppance that now I was obliged to move heaven and earth to keep her anchored to my side. If it was true that with age comes wisdom, I was going to have to live to be a hundred and twenty.

Although Nadia had dragged her feet over buying baby stuff, coming home laden with enough purchases to fill half the palazzo seemed to have made the impending birth real in her mind. Despite being slender and fit, over the last few days her bump had gone from a tidy football to something Santa Claus could envy. But there was a busyness about her that made me want to pull her down into a chair every time I saw her and say, 'Rest! Rest now! You won't get another chance.'

Instead, she appeared at my door grinning as though she'd won the lottery. 'You remember my friend Katerina, from school? She's assistant director for the stage lighting for *Romeo and Juliet* at the Terme di Caracalla. She didn't know I was back until yesterday, but she's brought me a welcome-home present – four tickets for tomorrow night.'

I loved ballet, but I still didn't manage to chase the panic of 'you're giving birth in less than two weeks and you want to sit in the ruins of Roman baths in thirty-five degrees of heat' off my face.

Nadia put her hand up. 'I'll be fine. It'll probably be my last night out for a while. And I love Bruno Beneventi. He's incredible. I saw him at the Royal Opera House a few years ago.'

'If you're sure you're up to it?'

'I am.' I couldn't put her under house arrest, though I was at the stage where I wanted to keep checking that the midwife was standing by her front door with her running shoes on and the ventouse packed.

Nadia said, 'It seems a bit churlish not to invite Annie. And it is pretty special to see a performance at Caracalla.'

My heart lifted at Nadia's friendly overture to Annie. I was long past the stage where I should be meddling in my daughter's friendships, but Nadia could benefit from spending time with people who were less organic grapes production and more Prosecco consumption. I knew, however, that any excess enthusiasm from me would kill off Nadia's, so I simply said, 'That would be very generous. I'm sure she'd love it. Who else will you invite?'

Nadia did a 'Who do you think?' sigh. 'Can you imagine us all heading off and leaving Marina behind?'

'I'm not sure she's a huge fan of ballet.'

Nadia shrugged. 'No. But she hates being left out more. And, to be fair, she was brilliant at organising Federico to take me to buy the baby things. You should have seen her bossing him about. I do owe her.'

So, the next night, we headed across Rome. Predictably, Nadia had refused to take a taxi on the grounds that travelling by train caused eighty per cent less greenhouse gas. We all had to suffer Marina announcing at frequent intervals that it was 'literally years' since she'd sullied herself with the metro. 'I'd rather go on the back of your mother's Vespa.'

I was too nervous that the ferocious jolting would dislodge Nadia's baby to have any energy left for Marina's dramatics and exited the boiling-hot carriage with great relief when we reached Circo Massimo. However, even I had to be thrilled we'd made the effort.

Annie's excitement about the venue was so British – 'I love outdoor performances. It's such a treat to take a warm evening for granted and not to have to factor in umbrellas and pac-a-macs in case it suddenly starts chucking it down.' Her delight went some way to assuage my guilt at setting her physical rather than cerebral tasks over the last ten days. I'd designed them to burn up her terrific energy and allow me the space to concentrate on my daughter. As always, Annie had welcomed every challenge, hiking up the Gianicolo Hill and along the Appian Way, proclaiming it excellent thinking time 'in the best scenery I could wish for'.

Tonight, she kept thanking Nadia for inviting her and then enthusing about the stage set against the backdrop of the arches of Roman ruins. 'This is absolutely magical. Stars as a roof! You couldn't have a more perfect location. I'll never want to go to the Albert Hall again.' She scanned the programme, exclaiming as she recognised the names in the cast, surprising me with her knowledge.

Even Marina stopped muttering about the hard seats and sank into a reverent silence when Bruno Beneventi floated onto stage. It didn't last long before she launched her commentary. 'Look at the muscles on his arms. Do you think he's stuffed a sock down his tights? How do they even get their legs up that high? He's picking her up as though she weighs no more than a newspaper.'

I was so torn between trying to shush Marina and keep an eye on Nadia, whose face was covered in a film of sweat, that it took me a while to realise that Annie was crying next to me. I put my hand on her leg. 'What's happened?'

She waved me away. 'Sorry, sorry, I find ballet really emotional.'

I hadn't put Annie in the category of 'reduced to tears by creative genius'. She'd always seemed a bit more pragmatic than that. Though we could all appreciate the delicate beauty of the two protagonists, who were so convincing that it was easy to forget they weren't two star-crossed lovers under a Roman sky, but two super-fit human beings who must have rehearsed who knew how many hours to deliver such a polished performance.

I didn't know whether to be embarrassed or alarmed when Annie's weeping took on a shuddering and sobbing quality that brought her to Marina's attention. She whispered to me – as much as Marina could whisper – something that roughly translated as 'What's she got to wail about?'

I pulled a face, annoyed that the one evening Nadia was relaxed and happy, someone else had popped up like a Jack-in-a-box of joy sucking. I patted Annie's knee and offered her a tissue, hoping she wasn't going to go full-on Stendhal syndrome and faint. My brain chose that moment to remember that a few years ago a visitor to the Uffizi in Florence had had a heart attack while admiring Botticelli's *Birth of Venus*. It would be wonderful to complete an evening of culture without requiring a defibrillator.

Annie crumpled next to me. 'My mum used to take me and my sister to the ballet.' Remorse washed over me for not considering whether there was something more at stake than appreciation of the perfect pas de deux.

I reached for her hand. 'Do you want to leave?' I asked, already dreading what Nadia would say if I went home with Annie.

'No. I'll get a grip in a minute. So sorry.'

Human beings were so messy with their timings. Annie had had every evening for nearly a month to realise she wasn't quite so blasé about her mother and sister as she thought. I had to believe this was progress, but I still wished it could have taken place in the confines of my palazzo. Somewhere I could make tea and focus fully rather than be caught on the hop when I was already praying not to hear the gush of Nadia's waters breaking.

I hardly dared peer down the row to see whether Nadia had noticed Annie unravelling. But she wasn't looking at us or even at the stage. Instead, she was grimacing and fidgeting in her seat. I reassured myself that my mobile was in my handbag, then tapped her on the shoulder. 'Are you okay?'

Nadia wrinkled her nose. 'Yes, fine. I'm just a bit uncomfortable. The seats aren't doing my back any favours.'

It was an insult to the glorious setting, the ancient ruins that were the perfect pink-lit backdrop to *Romeo and Juliet*, that I was on countdown to getting home. When Bruno Beneventi and his partner did their final bow, I could have pirouetted out of there on a wave of gratitude. It was truly a low bar for an evening's entertainment if the measure of success was returning home with the same number of people we came with – without exhausting our handkerchief supply.

Marina announced that there was no way she was taking the metro as her knees were killing her and for once, Nadia didn't argue.

I dropped back as we queued at the exit to check on Annie. 'Memories can pop up when you least expect them.'

'I didn't think it would get to me. It reminded me that my sister and I used to be a proper team. When we were younger, we always used to unite to handle my mother, but at some point, she managed to divide and rule. I miss that camaraderie, that sense that we might have been born into a difficult family but we still had each other.'

'Give her time to miss you. When she's had a chance to adjust to your mother's death, you might find she seeks you out of her own accord.'

Annie muffled a sob and I grappled for a distraction.

'Did you ever do ballet yourself?'

She took a breath. 'I had a few lessons because my mother

was interested in all sorts of dancing. I think she was hoping that one of us might take up ballet or tap. My sister showed quite a lot of promise when she was little, but, as my mother used to say, I had all the necessary strength but none of the grace.'

I wondered if parents would be that blunt nowadays. With Nadia, I'd always trusted that life would provide a reality check soon enough. There was no need to major on the fact that she was unlikely to make the Olympic sprinting team or see her artwork hang in the Galleria Nazionale. I hadn't felt obliged to extinguish dreams before they had even glittered on the horizon.

As we got into the cab, I said to Annie, 'Our trip talking about perspective did me good.' I paused. 'It was meant to help you, not me, but, actually, I hadn't really thought about how supportive my parents were when I wanted to go to university to read French. It wasn't a natural path for farmers' daughters back then. It's hard to believe now that when I graduated in 1970 you could still be asked to resign from your job if you got married.'

Nadia craned round from the front seat. 'Dad was always in favour of you working, wasn't he?'

'He was very supportive of my career,' I said, allowing Matteo's feminist credentials to pass uncontested. I squashed down the little flip of rebellion at this narrative, and resisted countering with the fact that he had no problem with me working as long as it didn't inconvenience him.

Annie moved the conversation on. 'Your parents must have been so proud of you, though. You must have been quite a rarity, a woman going to university in the sixties.'

'I probably was for a woman of my background. It never really occurred to me to see it like that. I saw it as an escape from being stuck on the farm for the rest of my life.'

It still hurt that my parents' pride had turned to shame. Out of habit, I looked up to the sky and said a silent sorry. Then I blurted out the first thing that came into my head to change the subject.

'Did your mother work?'

'Yes, she—' Annie stopped. 'She did a bit of this and that, nothing much to speak of.' She pressed her nose against the taxi window and started talking about how lovely the Castel Sant'Angelo was, lit up at night.

Again, I had the impression that Annie wanted to be open, wasn't a private person but was battling against her tendency to wear her heart on her sleeve. I was still contemplating what possible reason she could have to act like that with me – who was I going to tell her deep dark secrets to? – when we drew up at home in the taxi.

I was fiddling with the keys to the main door when Nadia gasped beside me.

'Are you all right?'

'I've got a dull ache in my stomach.'

There was a pause while we all did a collective wide-eye.

'You're not due for another thirteen days, are you?' I asked. 'Do you think you're in labour?'

Nadia's face marbled with pain. 'I don't know. I felt a bit uncomfortable at the ballet tonight.'

Marina clapped her hands. 'How exciting. I hope it doesn't turn out to be wind. You did eat rather a lot of artichoke at lunchtime.'

Nadia gritted her teeth. 'It's not wind.' She arched her back.

I fought the urge to shout about calling the midwife or to give in to my fear of all the many dramatic birthing scenarios I'd seen on TV over the years. I reminded myself that most babies, especially first babies, took ages to arrive.

'Why don't we sit you down in your apartment? If you're in labour, you'll start to get regular contractions.' I sounded more confident than I felt, recognising that my birthing knowledge owed more to cows than humans.

Annie went to take Nadia's arm, but she shook her off. 'I can manage.'

Nadia refused to settle on the sofa, preferring to pace about. Annie said, 'I'll disappear, unless there's anything I can help with?'

Nadia ignored her, rocking from side to side, blank-faced. Even in these circumstances, Nadia's rudeness still embarrassed me.

'Thank you, Annie,' I said. I turned to Nadia. 'Do you think we should put up that paddling pool thing? How long does that take? Annie could help with that.'

'It's called a birthing pool!' Nadia snapped. 'I don't even know whether I'm in labour yet. I don't want to get any germs in it by inflating it too early.'

Nadia and her germs. She always talked as though there was an invisible army of bacteria clomping across every surface searching for a place to fester. For someone who worried so much about the environment, she was a devil for washing tea towels and dishcloths like she was running a launderette.

Annie gave me a little wave and walked out, saying, 'Let me know if you need me.'

Marina inspected the pictures on the box. 'Not sure I'm going to have enough puff for that thing. Better get Annie back in here with her young lungs.' A bubble of hysterical laughter rose in my chest as I imagined Marina and I taking it in turns to blow, turning purple in the face.

Nadia looked like she might resort to a long string of expletives. 'It's not a bloody lilo! It has a pump, for goodness' sake!'

I passed her a glass of water. I risked asking, 'How are you feeling?'

'My back aches, but I don't think I'm in proper labour.' She groaned, folding over onto her knees.

'I think you are. Would it be worth calling the midwife and asking her advice?'

What I really meant was 'Tell her to leap in the car and get here in the next half an hour because I am way out of my depth.'

Nadia asked, 'Shouldn't I wait until my waters break?'

'I'd talk to her and see what she suggests. I've got the number here.' I didn't have my glasses on, so I tapped on several dud apps before I located my contacts list. Nadia practically snatched the phone out of my hand, stabbing at the screen. I nearly sank to the floor with relief when I heard the calm voice on the other end.

I kept eyeing the birthing pool box. I hoped we wouldn't end up hauling buckets of water from the sink with Nadia shivering in two inches at the bottom and puffing like a steam engine to hold the baby in long enough for us to fill it up.

Nadia stopped talking to make a deep guttural sound. How I hoped that midwife was grabbing everything she needed and bluelighting herself across Rome at this very moment. Nadia started pacing about, her speech fading in and out as she responded to the questions.

Eventually, she handed me back my phone. 'She'll ring me in a couple of hours to see how I'm doing and come when my waters break or the contractions are five minutes apart.'

That felt like it was cutting it a bit fine, but I knew better than to comment.

'Should we crack on with putting the pool up?'

Nadia agreed.

Marina sliced open the box with a kitchen knife and pulled out an emergency repair kit, waving it around and laughing. 'Let's hope your mum and I don't have to stand there with our thumb on a puncture when the baby's about to pop out.'

I choked back a giggle.

Nadia elbowed us out of the way, but not before Marina

picked up a scoop. 'What's this for? To scoop the baby out? It's a bit small, isn't it?'

Nadia scowled. 'That's in case I have a bowel movement during labour.'

The look on Marina's face was priceless. For once, she was shocked into silence.

Nadia straightened up and rested her hands in the small of her back. 'I'd rather do this on my own please.'

Marina was immediately contrite. 'Sorry, *cara*. I was simply trying to ease the tension. I won't say anything else.'

Nadia let out a low moan. 'Please, go to bed. You too, Mum. I just want to have a bit of peace to practise my breathing techniques.'

My stomach dropped with that sense of realising I'd played it all wrong by attempting to make light of what lay ahead. 'Are you sure? What about all this? And filling it with water? You can't be lugging buckets about when you're in labour.'

'Mum, there's a hose that attaches to the tap. I'll call you if I need anything.'

I had no choice but to leave. I paused on the threshold. 'Should I ring Grant?'

'No.'

My fierce and forceful daughter. Independent to the last.

14

I had some insight into what it was like for husbands back in the day before they were allowed into delivery rooms and had to pace up and down outside. Time crawled past. I heard the church clock strike midnight, one o'clock, two. I stepped out onto my terrace, cursing my slightly impaired hearing as I strained for any sounds from Nadia's apartment. I thought I heard the occasional groan, but I wasn't sure whether I was confusing it with the noise of late-night taxis going over a grating on the road outside. At two-thirty, I knocked on her door. She opened up, her face blotchy and tense.

'Darling, please let me stay with you. I'll sit in the corner and I won't say a word.'

She frowned and looked as though she was about to argue, then relented and said, 'You can go in the kitchen.'

I hurried through before she changed her mind, noting with relief that the birthing pool was ready, just as Nadia exclaimed behind me. 'I think my waters have broken.'

I flurried about, grabbing an armful of towels from the kitchen cupboard.

Nadia was looking at the trickle of liquid running down her

leg. 'It's not how you imagine it, is it? I was expecting it to be like a bucket of water.'

My very obvious question felt oddly taboo, but, in the end, the fear that I might have to deliver the baby gave me courage. 'Aren't you supposed to call the midwife now?' I asked, sending up a quick prayer to St Gerard, the patron saint of childbirth, squirming at the hypocrisy of my return to a reliance on divine intervention after an absence of nearly fifty years.

'I'm about to,' Nadia said, her expression contorting with discomfort.

I decided to offer to leave rather than be ejected. 'When she comes, I'll go, unless you'd feel more comfortable with me here.'

I still wasn't quite prepared for the gusto with which Nadia seized on my suggestion. 'Oh absolutely. You won't want to see me with my backside in the air.'

'I'm not worried about that, Naddy. You're my daughter.' I forced away the blow of rejection and continued with a calmness that I was nowhere near feeling. 'You've got to find whatever works for you – I don't know anyone who'd win a beauty contest giving birth. I pushed so hard with you, my eyes were bloodshot for weeks.' I smiled at the memory. 'You were so beautiful and I looked like a zombie.'

'I'd rather be able to concentrate on what the midwife is saying without you distracting me by panicking.'

It was so tempting to ask Nadia to name a single crisis when she'd seen me panic rather than figure out the best way to tackle it. To hear her speak, I was some doddery old fool who spun on the spot and combusted from stress if the going got tough. However, objecting to her view of me when her shoulders were up around her ears as she weathered another contraction was not my first priority despite the great prickle of injustice.

I filled up a jug of water and set down two glasses on the table. 'I can't wait to meet your son or daughter,' I said because it was true, but also to fill the silence, which held the weight of things unsaid. One of those meaty silences, the sort that fill a room with their presence before any momentous event. I'd felt it before – the interminable wait before the hearse turned up to escort my mother and me to Dad's funeral. The scratchy times whenever Nadia was flying back to England, when all the misunderstandings I'd intended to resolve were still hanging in the air. When I wanted to cling to her, to make everything right so we could part with a clean slate but also longing for the leaving bit to be over, so I could dominate rather than dread the pain of separation.

Eventually, the midwife, Loredana, arrived, a tiny wisp of a woman but whose every cell packed an energetic punch. She bustled in, efficient, whipping out her blood pressure monitor, listening to the baby's heartbeat and timing contractions. Nothing about her demeanour suggested she was worried. The glorious peace that someone who knew what she was doing would be here for the duration flooded through me. She asked Nadia who she planned to have present in the room for the birth.

'No one. Just you.'

The midwife did the whole eyebrow thing, which felt filled with judgement about what a crummy mother I must be if my daughter would choose to go through this huge life experience on her own rather than suffer my presence.

'Would you like some privacy now?' I asked, trying at least to clock up some kudos for not imposing myself where I wasn't wanted. 'I'm only down the corridor if you change your mind.'

Loredana nodded briskly.

I got up to leave, then ran over to Nadia. I hugged her, a fraction too long as I waited for the reward of a softening, a relaxing, anything that could allude to a hint of a future understanding between us. Nadia was as unbending as the horsehair bolster my parents used to have across their bed. She almost reared up in her haste to free herself from me and Loredana guided her towards the bedroom, ushering her in with a protective and excluding arm. There was no doubt that dealing with dodgy family dynamics was not part of her remit.

'Good luck, darling,' I shouted. 'I'll be cheering you on from next door.' I stopped and took a few steps back towards the bedroom.

Loredana glanced irritably over her shoulder.

'You will take care of her, won't you?' I asked.

'Of course. That's my job,' she said, as though I'd been questioning her professional credentials rather than delivering a clumsy declaration of love. I lost the nerve to say, 'And don't hesitate to call an ambulance if there are any problems.'

I closed the door gently behind me. History was repeating itself. In my time of crisis, my parents hadn't given me the support I needed so I'd cut off from them. Nadia and I were going the same way, but I couldn't fathom out what was required of me, what sort of help would make a difference. I scrabbled about in my memory bank, wondering when we'd morphed from being an averagely happy family to a loosely connected group of disgruntled human beings. The random recollection that surfaced was of Matteo and me, with Nadia when she was about twelve, cycling around the gardens of Villa Borghese in the spring sunshine. One of those unremarkable moments for the ordinariness of the activity, but standout for the lack of underlying tension, an equilateral triangle, with no one straining for freedom and pulling the rest of us out of sync. We had had good times once.

I decided now was not the moment to do a forensic investigation into when that all had shifted. I could attest that we'd been bumbling along reasonably happily when she was twelve. What about thirteen? Fourteen? Nineteen? What would I gain by pinpointing Nadia's age, the particular month, the offending year?

I passed by my apartment to call Strega, who scampered

outside, down the steps, delighted by the unexpected nocturnal adventure. We wandered into the relative cool of the garden. I leaned my forehead against the rough bark of the almond tree. The idea that it would have witnessed so many intergenerational dramas and still stood majestic and impervious to human idiocy comforted me.

When Nadia was born forty-two years ago, the wishes I'd harboured for her hadn't encompassed any notion of having to draw deep on her reserves to prove how strong she was. How resilient. How independent. I'd never fast-forwarded to a future in which her marriage would fail, though, to be fair, I'd never imagined her marrying someone quite so pompous either. And if I'd ever dreamt that one day she might provide me with grandchildren, I was pretty sure that Nadia choosing to give birth in the company of a stranger hadn't featured. One certainty I did have, however, was that I would be the one to sustain her through the vagaries of life. Oh the delusion of motherhood.

I sat on the bench, Strega hopping up beside me, my thoughts circling around the past, then back upstairs to the present, my heart straining for reassurance that my daughter was okay. The excitement at meeting my first grandchild was tinged with the fear derived from first-hand evidence that life can turn on a sixpence.

A couple of bats dived and dipped around the street light outside. On the warm night air, the scent of my roses, which always made me think of my mother's very English garden, mingled with wafts of uncollected rubbish. I sat there for ages, my mind skittering in disparate and unrelated directions – the diligence with which my dad used to tip the dustbin men at Christmas, the frequency with which I discovered maggots in Italian peaches, the idea that the constellations my teenage friends and I had gazed at during long Cornish summers were visible here, right above me.

I stared at the brightest star I could see, not sure whether it was the North Star, feeling ridiculous for wishing on it but doing so anyway. I asked for a safe arrival into the world for the next generation of our family. Then I pushed my luck by throwing in a request for finding a way to draw a line under everything that had gone before and to walk forwards with purpose into a new era.

My heart leapt as I heard the latch on the gate. Strega let out a little woof, then wagged her tail. It was Marina, an elegant ghost in a silk nightdress and negligee.

Her concern for me manifested itself in a diatribe in Italian, her language of the heart, insulting me for my stupidity of staying up all night.

'I can't sleep.'

'You haven't tried.' She passed me a mug of tea, a proper English brew, thick and soupy. 'I left the bag in.'

I smiled into the darkness. By Marina's standards, that was the ultimate concession, favouring as she did a disgusting milky slop.

'Did you hear anything from upstairs?' I asked.

'No. I didn't see any water swilling under the door when I went past, so I assume the paddling pool hasn't burst. Do you want to go up and see how they're getting on?'

'Want? Yes, absolutely. Will I? No.'

'I can't understand this ridiculous refusal to allow you to be with her,' Marina said.

I leapt to Nadia's defence, automatically. 'She's always been so self-sufficient. I almost wish Grant had come out. We might not like him but at least he'd be a familiar face.'

Marina snorted. 'Pah. He'd probably be moaning about how tired he was, being up all night, and how he might have a little nap but if they could call him for the main event...'

I had to laugh. Grant was a man who swore by his eight

hours but, despite sleeping better than the rest of us put together, was always knackered.

There we sat, all night, talking both nonsense and total sense. We speculated on how the world would change again in my grandchild's lifetime and reminisced about the things that had fallen out of fashion in ours. 'Do you remember the *gettoni*, the tokens we needed to make a call in a public phone box?' Marina asked.

'I used to stockpile them when I first moved out here. It's hard to believe that young people don't even bother getting a landline now,' I said. 'They were simpler times. Would you do anything differently if you could do it all over again?'

Marina patted my leg. 'Life can only be understood backwards, but it must be lived forwards.'

'That's very philosophical.' And most unlike Marina, who never usually missed an opportunity to curse her ex-husbands.

'I know. I saw it in the newspaper a year or so ago when there was that conference here about that chap, you know the one who was into existentialism, that Danish theologian/philosopher, nineteenth century. He said it.'

'Can't help you there,' I said, noticing that pink and golden streaks were stretching across a lightening sky.

'Søren Kierkegaard!' Marina said, making Strega growl at her shout of triumph.

'None the wiser, but you've always been cleverer than me. Great quote, though, it's a good mantra.'

And we sat in silence, a different kind from earlier, the sort between friends that feels spangled with understanding, with their best and warmest memories of you, threaded through with an imperfect but enduring love.

15

Fowey, Summer 1975

Eddie had announced just before the beginning of the summer holidays that his ex, Nancy, wasn't around for the next six weeks, so the girls would have to stay with me in Cornwall. He'd spend as many days down here as possible, but, inevitably, he'd still be away for a good chunk of the time.

'Where's she off to?' I asked, irritated that Eddie, and probably Nancy as well, had taken for granted that I'd step into the breach to look after their daughters.

'Does it matter?' He scowled. 'She's got a tour come up. Last minute.'

'Who's going to look after them when I'm working at the library?'

'I told you not to tie yourself down with that job. You'll have to give it up, at least for the summer.'

My instinctive reaction burst out before I could find the one that would keep the peace. 'No. Your wife can turn down whatever she's accepted. They're not my responsibility.'

Eddie's face tightened. Not far behind came that familiar tensing in my chest, as though my soul was adopting a brace position for what I knew would come later.

I added, 'Much as I love them' and heard myself blathering on about sorting something out, swapping shifts, seeing if I could have a few days off unpaid.

But Eddie didn't reply, didn't try to meet me halfway. Simply spent the rest of the weekend picking fault with how I'd cooked the chicken, made our bed, ironed his shirts. It was a relief when he left for London without his bad mood escalating into something much darker. It happened rarely, but often enough to teach me to measure my words and watch my back.

A little scintilla of rebellion was igniting in me, like the spark wheel on an empty lighter, showing willing but not yet managing to produce a flame. It refused to fade away completely, though. Since I'd started working at the library, giving myself a purpose and routine, I was so much happier. The job wasn't intellectually challenging but I loved being surrounded by novels and words. My horizons had expanded outwards simply by mixing with different people on a daily basis, although I still craved an opportunity to travel and use my French.

As nothing more was said about it, I assumed that Nancy had decided not to go on her tour. Then one Thursday night in July I returned home and my heart leapt at the unexpected sight of Eddie's car. The girls flew down the steps to greet me. Heather threw her arms over my shoulders and hung with her feet off the floor.

'Helloooo! I didn't know you were coming today,' I said, delighted to see them despite my frustration at how often their mother took advantage of me.

Heather whispered, 'We're not supposed to tell you, but we're staying for the whole of the summer holidays.'

I snapped my head round to see Eddie standing at the front door. He was all smiles. 'We thought we'd surprise you.'

Heather finally released me and I bent down to give Lyndsey a kiss on her head.

She was wide-eyed. 'Don't tell Daddy what Heather said.'

Heather was busy hopscotching up the path, apparently not the least bit worried about the ramifications of spilling the secret.

I could practically feel my blood boiling. I had no one to rely on, no one who could look after the children while I was at work. I stomped up the steps. Eddie pulled me towards him and kissed me hard until I felt my lips bruise against my teeth. I wriggled free.

'What's wrong with you?'

'I gather the girls are here for the summer.'

His eyes flashed towards Heather, then he focused on me again, smiling and holding his hands up. 'I'm sorry, there was a bit of a misunderstanding with Nancy. I thought she'd cancelled, but she flew to the States this morning.'

I stared at him. I could feel the disbelief swamping my face, reflecting my fury at his breathtaking arrogance, this expectation that everyone else should do whatever they wanted and good old Ronnie would pick up the slack.

A thought buzzed in my head with the insistent thrum of a summer lawnmower. After four years, I finally had to admit the truth that I'd been attempting to deny as Eddie's behaviour had become more erratic and cruel. Eddie didn't care about me. This wasn't love. Or, if it was, it was a peculiar and selfish version of it.

In my mind, I elbowed him out of the way. In reality, I smiled weakly, squeezed past him and stamped through to the kitchen. I ran the tap until the water was ice cold. I was taking a gulp, the freezing liquid slipping down my throat, a contrast to the hot anger raging around my body, when I heard a commotion in the hallway. I shot through to find Heather, her hands shielding her head as Eddie went at her with his belt. 'You stupid little sod. I told you I would deal with it. I told you not to say anything.'

In my peripheral vision, I saw Lyndsey sitting on the stairs, staring down at her book as though she was reading, but her face twitched with every crack of the belt.

I grabbed at Eddie. I'd never seen him lose his temper like this with the children before. 'Get off her. Get off!'

He pushed me backwards, but I steadied myself on the wall and snatched at the belt. We struggled in a tug of war. Heather was crying, her face mottled with fear and shock, a big welt across one cheek.

'Go upstairs,' I shouted. 'Take Lyndsey with you.'

Heather grabbed her five-year-old sister by the arm. Lyndsey scampered into her bedroom, but Heather hesitated halfway up, her little chest heaving as Eddie pushed his hand into my face, trying to loosen my grip. 'Don't hit Ronnie. She might leave you as well. Mummy's already said if you slap her again, she'll divorce you.'

Eddie's hands went slack for a moment and I seized my opportunity to take control of the belt.

Heather gasped at the audacity of her words and stampeded off, with Eddie storming after her. She was too quick for him and locked herself in the bathroom. She screamed as he kicked at the door.

I threw the belt in the understairs cupboard and ran upstairs. 'Eddie! Eddie! Calm down. Stop it!'

'She is not going to get away with cheeking me like that. She has no idea what she's talking about. She's just trying to make trouble.'

'Give it a rest. You're scaring her. She's eight years old, for goodness' sake. She's only repeating what she's heard.'

To my relief, Eddie's body relaxed. As he moved away from the door, tucking in his shirt and straightening his sleeves, my panic subsided enough to process what Heather had said.

My determination to understand exactly what was going on outweighed my fear of his reaction. For the moment, anyway. 'When did Nancy say that? Recently? Why? I thought your divorce was nearly through anyway?' As the questions tumbled out of me, I despised myself for skating round the bigger issue of Eddie – charismatic, generous Eddie – resorting to a smack, a fist in the stomach, a painful twist of the arm for any woman who didn't immediately see things his way.

He stepped towards me. I flinched. 'Hey,' he said, suddenly turning on the warmth as though the spring sunshine was emerging after an April storm. 'I've been wanting to talk to you about Nancy. She has this crazy idea that I'm back living with her because I've stayed over a few nights to make sure the girls are safe when she's had too much to drink.'

'What? You've slept at your ex-wife's house without mentioning it to me?'

I watched his expression vacillate. The battle between the Eddie who drew me close to dance to Barry White's 'You're the First, the Last, My Everything' and the man who blamed his smack to my face on his passion for me, the strength of his feelings that meant he couldn't always control himself.

The first time, a year or so ago, beneath the shock, there'd been the surprise that I could stir such emotions in a man, a proper grown-up, well into his thirties. Of course I'd forgiven him. Even accepted that it was my fault for winding him up. Every time it happened, I thought about leaving him. And then he'd apologise and explain how difficult Nancy was being about the divorce. How frustrated he was when all he wanted to do was make a life with me. If I could just hold on for another year or so, he'd be free. And, really, what was another twelve months in comparison to our glorious future ahead?

But on the last couple of occasions, my heart had hardened. Ideas of a life without him had begun to seep into my daydreams. But where would I go? I couldn't imagine turning up at the farm with my suitcase, Mum glancing down the road to see if anyone had seen me slinking home, her mouth twitching with all the 'told you so's she'd been fermenting and curating over the last four years.

His fingers closed around the top of my arm. I shook him off, but he grabbed the nape of my neck. I whimpered and he jabbed me in the kidneys. Squealing, I tried to swivel round, but he held me tight by my hair, swearing in my ear about what I could expect if I didn't stop doing his head in with questions.

I heard the click of the bathroom door, then saw the flash of Heather's flowery T-shirt as she slipped behind Eddie and pummelled her fists on his back. 'Let her go! Dad! Get off Ronnie!' I managed to get a kick into his shins and he lost his footing, landing heavily on his side. I didn't stop to check whether he was okay. I tugged at Heather's hand and we ran, fleeing down the stairs and along the hallway. I scrabbled at the front door, my fingers refusing to co-operate before bursting out into the fresh air, astonished that the world was still out there. The sun was shining, the wild gladioli flashed bright pink as we flew past, the orange Californian poppies nodded a lazy greeting as our feet clattered along the tarmac and down to the beach, my ears straining for the thud of footsteps behind us.

Heather and I huddled on the sand, next to a couple of men in deckchairs about my dad's age, sipping beer from cans. They had kindly faces, craggy and solid, men who might intervene if Eddie turned up.

I tried, really hard, not to cry. 'Can you stay here? I need to go back for Lyndsey. Promise me you won't move.'

Heather patted my hand. 'Dad won't hurt Lyndsey. He

never does. Just Mum.' She turned away, her eyes drifting to the sea and scanning the horizon as though she was waiting for a sailboat to appear. 'And me.' Those last two words broke me. I'd been fooling myself that Eddie's anger sometimes tipped into physical aggression because it was the flipside of his infatuation with me. I ached with sorrow that Heather had already learnt to assess the danger represented by the very person who should have protected her.

I knew then that the love I'd had for Eddie wasn't enough. That this dazzling fever of feelings had dwindled to embers that would no longer be capable of generating a flame. That I could never again forgive a man who took his temper out on this ferocious and brave little girl, whose eight-year-old heart was so full of courage that she was prepared to risk Eddie's wrath to save me.

For now, though, I had to keep us all safe over the summer while I figured out what to do.

16

Present Day

By eight o'clock, Marina had gone for a sleep. Annie had disappeared on one of her crack-of-dawn walks to Piazza Navona and the Pantheon before the tourists arrived. The squeal of brakes on the road outside, the *motorini* labouring up the hill and the rumble of the buses heralded a new day. An ordinary day for many, but potentially a life-changing one for me.

I hovered outside Nadia's door. I could hear a voice, the midwife's, low and calm, but no corresponding noise from Nadia. My whole body longed to be on the other side of the wall, reassuring myself that none of the things my evil imagination conjured up were happening. My ability to assume the best in any stressful situation had expired in 1976.

I went into my apartment to fetch some water. I would knock in half an hour: not bothering them for a whole night was more than acceptable. As I filled a glass, I heard a door open, so I peeked out into the hallway.

The midwife was all smiles. She threw her arms up. '*Congratulazioni! Lei è diventata nonna!*'

I didn't wait to be invited. I raced along the corridor and burst in to find Nadia lying on the sofa in a nightshirt with a bundle clutched to her chest. I made myself slow down. I grasped her hand. 'Oh thank goodness. You're all right. Oh bless you. What did you have?'

Nadia smiled, the dazed but delighted expression of someone who'd had no idea what would be required of her body. 'A little girl. Flora.'

'Flora. Perfect. Just perfect. Can I look at her?'

Nadia shifted position and peeled the towel back. I'd always dismissed babies as resembling pink piglets, half of them over-cooked with ruddy faces and squashed boxer noses. But as I looked down at my granddaughter's tufts of dark hair, her long eyelashes and pouty little mouth, I knew that I was destined to become the absolute *nonna* cliché and fall straight into the trap of thinking she was the most beautiful baby that ever sucked in oxygen.

'Naddy. She's utterly gorgeous. Were you all right? Did she come out okay?'

Nadia nodded. 'No stitches at least. You'd think that bodies would have evolved to make childbirth a bit easier by now.'

The midwife came back in and told me how quick the birth was, how wonderful Nadia had been, what a good weight Flora was, despite being a bit early.

I pulled up a chair and inspected Flora's tiny fingernails, the waxy creases in the soles of her feet, marvelling that nature provided for all those things in miniature, growing them inside another human being.

'Marina and I have been up all night waiting for news. She's just gone to bed.'

A flicker of annoyance passed over Nadia's face. 'Why didn't you go to sleep?'

I might have known that I'd fail my birth etiquette test, but I grinned. Nothing was going to spoil this moment. 'I was too excited.' I left off 'and worried about you'. If Nadia and I shared one character trait, it was that we hated people fussing around us.

Every bit of me wanted to sit and watch Flora breathe in and out and pester the midwife for reassurance that mother and baby were in rude health, especially as I'd dared to glance over to the vacated birthing pool, which was a mistake I wouldn't make a second time.

Instead, I touched Flora's head and asked, 'Shall I leave you to rest?'

Nadia said, 'Why don't you go and have a sleep, then come back with Marina this afternoon?'

I said my goodbyes, clutching the invitation to me like a delicate butterfly that I might squash in my enthusiasm to keep it safe.

'Love you. Love you both,' I said.

After the initial elation and the flurry of phone calls to my friends, the night without sleep and the accompanying mixture of excitement and fear took its toll. Over the next few days, I felt every one of my seventy-four years. My bedroom was directly underneath Nadia's apartment and I could either hear the baby crying, or thought I could, but didn't dare offer to help anywhere near as much as I wanted to. Nadia had been very specific in her instructions that 'just because I live opposite doesn't mean you can pop in and out willy-nilly. I need time to bond with her without a whole barrage of advice.'

I slipped in a couple of times during the day. I brought plates of pasta and mugs of tea, resisting uttering the suggestions that were surging and swooping in my head like swifts at dusk. I smiled. I nodded. I cradled and rocked. I shut my mouth. Nadia's euphoria of having delivered a healthy baby was slowly giving way to the shock of understanding that she was – and would be for the foreseeable future – at the beck and call of a tiny dictator, who refused to listen to reason. A terrifying new world where university degrees, seniority at work, ability to speak two languages fluently counted for naught. Nadia was a woman who thrived on order and control. Relying on me as her only option to use the bathroom without the wails of a baby sending her stress levels soaring hadn't been part of her road map.

In daylight hours, I could talk myself down from tapping at her door more than strictly necessary for shower duty (allowed) and lunch provision (tolerated). But it was night-time when I itched to go to her. I still remembered the relentlessness of finishing an interminable cycle of feeding, winding and changing, finally dropping off before a cry would drag me back up again. At two, three, four a.m., I dithered outside Nadia's door, the baby's screaming acting like some kind of visceral tow rope. Fear of copping the blame later on for preventing Nadia bonding with her baby stopped me from intruding.

But four days after Flora's birth and following a good half an hour of yelling that was increasing in volume, I knocked gently at quarter to five in the morning. There was no reply, so I contravened all 'adult daughter living in her mother's apartment block' boundaries and let myself in with my own key. I was braced for an onslaught, but the fight had gone out of Nadia, who was slumped in a chair, tears streaming down her face, jiggling her tiny daughter. 'Why is she still crying? I've changed her nappy, I've fed and winded her, but she won't go to sleep. Every time the midwife has checked up on us, she says everything is fine but this can't be normal. What am I doing wrong?'

For once, I had the sensation that my presence was mildly

welcome. 'You're not doing anything wrong. Babies sometimes become overtired and can't get themselves off. Would you like me to hold her?' I picked up the sweaty little body writhing and shrieking in Nadia's arms. 'Come here, come to Nonna. Why don't you have a lie-down for a bit? I can walk around with her. Shall I take her down into the garden where it's cooler? She's perhaps hot.'

Nadia looked uncertain. 'You won't trip on the steps outside, will you?'

Nadia clearly saw me as a clumsy old relic who would choose this moment to fall down a flight of stairs after never doing so in the forty-odd years I'd lived here. Still, it was reassuring that her maternal instincts were operating as they should be, primed to protect.

'No, I will go really slowly and carefully. I promise I'll call you if she needs feeding.'

I let Strega out and she pattered along, excited at this excuse for an early outing. I hummed 'Jerusalem' into the baby's head, feeling the notes vibrate in my chest and throat. Still Flora screamed. I willed her to be quiet so that Nadia could trust me and get some sleep.

'And did those feet in ancient time, Walk upon England's mountains green? And was the holy Lamb of God, On England's pleasant pastures seen?'

I marvelled over the fact that I'd defaulted to a patriotic British hymn, long buried in my psyche from school assemblies, the words a reflex rather than a memory.

Backing out of the front door, a cotton sheet over my shoulder, I noted the one-handed, left-buttocked skill of motherhood returning like an old friend I hadn't seen for years but in whom I still had complete faith. I went down the steps and opened the gate to my patch of garden at the side of the house. Marina teased me, but I kept the lawn green by hurling washing-up water, dregs of tea and coffee leftovers onto the grass from my balcony. It was a habit I'd adopted during the infamous drought of 1976. That terrible summer when my shame blazed as brightly as the·sunshine. I'd stayed inside the farmhouse, venturing outside only to empty the washing-up bowl onto our crispy lawn, not even wanting to stumble across the labourers, to see their pity or disdain. My father, usually philosophical and stoic, had been short-tempered and tetchy, living in fear of his fields catching fire while the combine harvesters jammed up with ladybirds and aphids. Or maybe that's what I put it down to, unable to take on the responsibility of more guilt than I carried already.

In Rome, though, I'd become accustomed to summers of searing, insistent heat. I'd learnt to enjoy the predictability of endless good weather. I put the sheet onto the grass under the gnarly olive tree in the corner and laid Flora down. Her mouth was a perfect hollow of indignation. I peeled off her vest and, after hesitating for a moment, took off her nappy, letting her kick freely in the balmy morning air. I stretched out beside her, smoothing her eyebrows, those magnificent scowling hyphens of disapproval. Strega sat at my feet, occasionally emitting a brief whimper of bemusement.

I glanced up expecting to see Nadia peering over the wall of her terrace, assessing whether I was sensible enough to stop the dog from smothering the baby. But nothing.

Slowly, in a way that I would always find magical, Flora's cries subsided, her tiny blue-veined eyelids flickering half-shut, then flying open as though she needed to keep watch for wolves.

'I'm here,' I whispered, letting her fold her hand around my finger.

I sat up, hearing the church bell strike five, the pink and orange of the sky already shifting to blue.

Strega nudged my elbow for a stroke. I reached out to rub her furry stomach, my motions slow so as not to disturb Flora. I stared down at my granddaughter, lyrical observations about the miracle of life burning within me in a way that felt both poetic and grandiose. Almost as though I had woken up to an understanding of the magic of parenthood – or grandparenthood – that everyone else had cottoned on to years ago. I studied Flora's face for traces of Nadia, of Grant. Apart from her dark eyebrows and pointed chin, which were all Nadia, she was just Flora, a unique little being.

I'd intended not to get too close, to protect myself against the possibility of Nadia disappearing back to England with her. But in the space of a few days, I'd recklessly abandoned everything I'd learnt about the incompatibility of love and the preservation of heart.

For the first time in forever, an ancient image of the two children who'd wormed their way into my affection when I was young enough to love without hesitation popped into my mind. One sweet and anxious to please, the other mischievous and boisterous, their little faces bursting with the ready smiles and energy of youth. I'd embraced them with a freedom and nonchalance that I'd understood later came from knowing they had their own mother. I'd had the luxury of believing that what I did or didn't do wouldn't matter. Or so I'd thought. I'd never even had the opportunity to say goodbye, to hug them one last time.

Over the next hour, I let my mind wander back to my arrival in Rome. I even allowed my thoughts to stray to the day of the crash, an act of self-sabotage I usually resisted with all my might. Nearly fifty years later, the memories still engendered a surge of panic. I calmed myself by staring down at Flora. I touched her cheek to check she wasn't too hot. Her little body twitched. I stiffened, relaxing again as she settled on the sheet. I battled to focus on her but the past tightened its grip, sucking me into recollections of the two fraught years at home with my parents following the accident. I'd paid a daily penance, witnessing the recriminations on my mother's face. I'd endeavoured to make amends and even resigned myself to staying to help Dad on the farm. It hadn't been enough. After a particularly bruising row about the shame I'd brought on the family and another diatribe about how no man would ever want me as if that was the be all and end all, I'd planned my escape.

I took the first job I could find abroad, which happened to be a housekeeper in Italy. I forced myself to concentrate on the future, blocking out thoughts of home. I even confounded my mother's dire warnings about never finding a husband, marrying Matteo two years later. I'd hoped Nadia's arrival soon afterwards was a definitive line in the sand, when I could consign all that trauma to the past. The decades contradicted me, showing that I'd carried the chaos with me, held back, kept Nadia at arm's length, afraid to risk loving, afraid of not measuring up, afraid of failing to do the right thing when it mattered.

Now here I was. With a daughter I was trying to forgive for her tacit acceptance of Matteo's behaviour. A daughter who didn't appear to like me and to whom I didn't know how to build a bridge.

I watched Flora's chest rise and fall. It was a lot to ask of a baby who wasn't even a week old to be the life raft that transported us from one side to the other.

The latch rattled on the garden gate. I glanced around to see Annie and put my finger to my lips.

She crept over and sat down. 'You're about early.'

'Nadia's been up all night. I wanted her to have a nap. I can still remember that feeling of total exhaustion.'

Annie smiled. 'She's so lucky to have you. My mother was entirely uninterested in my boys. She paid far more attention to my sister's girls, my nieces. She improved a bit when they were teenagers and they could help her sort out the Wi-Fi.' I loved the way Annie's face softened when she talked about her sons.

'Can you just keep an eye on Flora while I nip to the loo? I've been desperate for the last hour.'

'Sure. No worries.'

I scuttled off, with Strega following. By the time I returned, I could hear voices in the courtyard.

Nadia was shouting and grabbing at Flora. She rounded on me. 'I can't trust you, can I? You said you wouldn't take your eyes off her and I come down and you've dumped her on Annie.'

'Nad. Naddy. I needed a wee. I've been out here for nearly two hours. Annie was with her for five minutes. I didn't leave her with a random stranger.'

Annie was holding her hands up. 'Sorry, sorry. She woke up and started crying as soon as you left, Ronnie, so I picked her up to comfort her.'

I waved an okay at her and crossed over to Nadia. 'Darling. Annie was trying to help. We both were. I wouldn't leave Flora with anyone who wasn't completely trustworthy.'

Nadia had that glazed look about her, as though only the barest survival instincts were functioning.

'Why don't you give her a feed – the heat does make babies thirsty – and then try to have another sleep? It's torture that precisely when your body has been through so much, your hormones are all over the place and you really need a rest, the baby requires your attention.'

Nadia wasn't having any of it. 'No. You didn't do what you promised. You never ever do. I'm taking her with me.'

With perfect timing, Marina flashed through the gate, an early-morning vision in a purple kimono and bendy rubber rollers. 'What's going on here?'

Before I could say a word, Annie spoke.

'I'm sorry I picked up your baby, Nadia, but I just did what came naturally. I was actually thinking about your mum – I know she's in great shape for her age, but she's been up most of the night too. It's not so out of order for her to pop to the bathroom, for goodness' sake. Everything your mother does is geared towards making things easier for you and Flora. I could never have turned up at my mother's unannounced and had a welcome like she's given you.' Annie was gentle in her tone, but there was no dodging the unspoken, 'So stop being so flaming ungrateful'.

I wavered between applauding Annie for saying what I would never dare and being outraged that an outsider had the audacity to point out faults in my offspring that I acknowledged but hoped had slipped under everyone else's radar.

Childbirth hadn't dulled Nadia's reactions. 'I'm not sure I'm very interested in the opinion of someone who's freeloading from two batty old women who think they're somehow the messiahs of the menopausal. If you think my mother's so marvellous, feel free to help yourself.'

I couldn't think, couldn't find any joined-up words that might calm Nadia down. It was as though someone half my height had run full pelt into my stomach and knocked the air out of me with such force that I felt sick.

Marina threw back her head. 'Messiahs of the menopausal. That's brilliant!' She clapped her hands, startling Flora, who began to scream. 'Sorry, sorry,' Marina said as she clocked my face. 'You are a bit harsh, Nadia,' she remarked between splutters of suppressed laughter.

Nadia glowered at her and turned to exit the garden. She lumbered with the slow movements of someone who no longer trusted their nether regions not to expel liquid or unexpectedly drop a couple of inches, a bit like an aircraft flashing up a warning that the undercarriage wasn't securely attached.

Annie's face tightened. I finally managed to connect a couple of synapses long enough to raise a warning hand, but it was too late. Annie's voice growled out, 'Your mother is marvellous.'

Dread enveloped me. Nadia was not a woman to back into a corner. She hovered in the gateway, bobbing Flora up and down, shushing her, her face flickering between tenderness and something that was hard and hurtful. 'What do you even know about her? You're the oracle after one month? Try growing up with her. The woman you can never read, who always hovers just out of reach. No wonder my dad had an affair for all those years!'

Annie stepped back. 'Wow.' Her gaze flickered towards me. 'Wow.' She sounded nearly as winded as I was. 'If we're talking perspective, I'm astounded by yours, Nadia. Your mum is one of the warmest women I've ever met.'

Even Marina was silent.

I wasn't sure my poor sore heart could withstand any more truth. 'Shall we leave my shortcomings there?' I tried to make a joke through the mass of tears that were clogging my throat. 'We can revisit this theme another day at our leisure.'

Annie crossed over to me and put her hand on mine. 'I don't recognise that picture of you. You always go the extra mile to connect with people and make them welcome.'

Nadia lifted Flora up to her shoulder. 'You've no idea.'

Annie folded her arms and faced Nadia. 'I do know what I'm talking about. It's because of your mother that I understand what love and protection look like. She was the only person I could rely on when I was younger.'

The triple chorus of 'What?' reverberated around my little garden, but I knew, a visceral, instinctive knowing, before my brain patchworked the truth together.

Annie swung round to me. 'Ronnie, I'm sorry, I hadn't even decided whether I was going to tell you. I really didn't want to do it like this.'

There'd be a price to pay. In terms of smoothing things over with Nadia, this would be the sun through a magnifying glass that ignited further fury. But with the force of water over a weir after weeks of rain, happiness and shock flooded through me.

'Heather!' I hugged her. 'I never expected to see you again.'

17

Cornwall, January 1976

The summer had drifted into autumn and then Christmas was on the horizon and I was still stuck, unable to come up with a plan to save myself without abandoning the girls. Heather had given me her mother's number in London – 'Don't tell Dad I gave it to you.' I'd tried to talk to Nancy in November when Eddie was in France for the release of Beaujolais Nouveau. She'd sworn at me down the phone and hung up.

Out of desperation, I'd attempted to pave the way for returning to live with my parents, visiting a little more often and training myself to ignore my mother's barbed comments – 'That man's onto a good thing. Don't you come running to me if he gets you in the family way.' Every time I went, I was full of resolve, determined to swallow my pride and confess I was out of my depth. However, their disappointment was already so palpable that my nerve to admit the truth kept failing me. After a fraught Christmas, though, when Eddie had taken full advantage of his holiday to drink more than usual, I'd decided to catch a train up to London in the new year. I'd force Nancy to see me, to understand that I had her daughters' best interests at heart. If she met me, if she realised that I was willing to do anything to help, maybe I could still be part of their lives – their new lives, without Eddie.

I planned to go the following week when Eddie was away. The fear that he would discover what I was up to terrified me, but I drew courage from Heather, who bore the brunt of Eddie's bad moods with remarkable resilience.

As I drove us back from the pub in early January, two days before the start of the school term, Eddie was slurring his words and moaning about how badly behaved the girls were. I kept quiet, fighting a feeling that I couldn't trust my judgement, that my instinctive sense of right and wrong had eroded over the last four and a half years.

Afterwards, I kept remembering my eyes reflecting in the rear-view mirror. Urgent, desperate, pleading glances, willing the kids to do what Eddie said. To stop singing, to toe the line in a way that would halt the rising thrum of tension engulfing me. Gusts of stale cider wafted over with every little beat of his frustration at the tuneless, shouty rendition of 'Mamma Mia'. In the end, he'd lost it. 'Stop it! Just shut up! You're doing my nut in, both of you.'

Lyndsey fell silent, huddling into the corner of the back seat, well-versed in catching Eddie's tone and knowing when to become invisible. Heather, defiant and daring, leaned further forward, belting out the words into a pretend microphone.

I drove, the wipers of the BMW struggling to make headway against the thick sleet blowing in off the English Channel. Every sinew of my neck was taut with anxiety and concentration as I peered through the fog of the windscreen, which no amount of heat from the fan seemed to clear properly.

For a moment, Eddie turned on me. 'Put your foot down! I could run faster than this!'

'It's icy out there.'

'Pull over. Let me drive. I want to be back in time for *The High Chaparral*.'

'Eddie, I don't think that's a good idea. It's okay, I'll get you there. I'll go a bit faster. We'll be home in half an hour.'

He gripped my arm. 'Are you saying I'm too drunk to drive?'

'You're always a great driver,' I said, 'but it's high time I had a bit more practice in this car, you said it yourself. I'm still getting used to it.'

I breathed out as Eddie's fingers loosened, accelerating as much as I dared to keep him happy.

From behind, Heather gave an off-key squeal of Donna Summer's 'Love to Love You Baby' and Eddie's jaw tightened.

I was having to act as a buffer between the two of them more often, especially since Eddie's boss had promoted his own son over him. When I spoke to Heather about not antagonising him, she nodded. 'I know. I need to keep my thoughts in my head.' But the very next day, she'd point out how unfair he was, the inconsistencies in what he said, and the temperature would rise again, bringing with it wallops and bruises. I couldn't do it forever. I would be thirty in three years' time and if I didn't get out soon, my mother would indeed be able to take grim satisfaction in the knowledge that I had wasted the best years of my life.

'No!' I shouted, as Eddie pushed himself up in his seat, turning to silence Heather's singing with the force of his hand. Those hands that could caress and delight on a good day. I could never relax into those caresses any more. I knew how quickly everything could change. I grabbed at his sleeve. 'Eddie, don't.'

As he shoved me off, he knocked the steering wheel. The car swerved wide round a corner. A slap rang out, Eddie out of his seat, his hip against my shoulder as I wrestled for control, realising too late that I'd caught some black ice. The white-washed wall of a cottage loomed all too fast, too quickly for me to scream. To do anything other than cover my head as bits of brick and concrete rained down onto the bonnet and a van travelling too fast skidded into us, ploughing into the passenger side. I just had time to register the unnatural angle of the body in the striped jumper in the rear before the force of the impact flung Eddie forwards against the windscreen with a sickening crack. He fell on me, the weight of him pinning me against the door.

Then that single scream from the back seat. All my mistakes, all the times I should have been brave and fled with Heather and Lyndsey, distilled down into a moment awash with something way beyond fear. I struggled to free myself, my hands slippery with blood, frantic to see if the girls were all right. I was shouting their names, scrubbing at my face to clear my vision, panic taking command of my limbs and thoughts.

Within minutes, there was a melee of voices, my brain working hard to distinguish between the falsely cheery tones designed to reassure and the unguarded exclamations of shock and gasps of horror. The blasts of freezing air as faces leaned in and faded out, hands touched, patted, held and soothed. The sobbing that I was powerless to stem, not sure whether it was coming from me or someone else. Words that took shape in my head but couldn't make it out of my mouth. Then blue lights spinning, picking out the white of the frost on the tops of the stone walls and illuminating the side of Eddie's head, his dark hair matted into a clump.

I gave myself over to the capable instructions that filled the car, the people that moved with the confidence of knowing what helped and what hindered.

'The girls? Eddie?' I managed to croak out.

'The seat belts did their job in the back,' an ambulance man said, before turning to give orders to his colleagues. 'Well done for making the girls wear them. We're taking you all to the hospital to get you checked out now.'

But even in my fuddled state, I heard the omission, the thing unsaid, the unbearable fact that everyone was postponing to a later date. I was twenty-seven years old and I'd killed someone when I was driving.

18

Present Day

'Anyone mind explaining to the elderly stateswoman in the curlers what the heck is going on? I'm feeling as though I've come in on episode five of those box sets you were so keen on in the pandemic, Ron.' Marina brandished her walking cane in mock remonstrance.

I pressed my fingers into my eyes, but I couldn't stop the tears pouring out. Annie kept spluttering between sobs and laughter.

In all the scenarios I'd barely dared to imagine over the years, I'd always envisaged the two – or perhaps three – of us rushing at each other with a wild delight, unconstrained and pure. Instead, in my peripheral vision, there was Nadia. With my granddaughter, the child with whom I longed to have a relationship, one that my mistakes wouldn't taint. An uncomplicated bond, simple and linear. Judging by the clouds scudding across Nadia's face, the way she hugged Flora close as if to protect her from the imperfections of her grandmother, this latest revelation wouldn't advance my case.

'This is one long story,' I said, not yet ready to scrape back the layers of what would have to be laid bare. The bits of the past that I'd tucked away, allowing scar tissue to form over the raw wounds, were squeezing in, making me dizzy with their potency.

'The suspense is killing me, Ron. How long is this story? Am I going to live long enough to hear the end of it?' Marina peered closely at me. 'Here, sit in the shade at the table for a minute. Annie, go and get some water.'

I sat down and Annie scurried off.

Nadia slid into a chair next to me and in between fumbling to latch Flora onto a breast, said, 'So you knew Annie from before? And it's taken you all this time to realise that it's her? Let me get this straight. A random woman applied to come and live here and, ooh, massive coincidence, you were so important to her when she was younger but you didn't recognise her or her name? Where do you even know her from? Are you sure she's not making up some weird story to scam you?'

Marina took a seat, frowning. 'We chose her together. I did the paperwork and took her passport details. I commented on the fact she was called Heather, not Annie. She was very clear that she hated the name Heather and she went by her middle name of Anne, or rather Annie, which she preferred. I didn't think any more about it. Certainly didn't bother mentioning it to Ronnie.'

I could see where Nadia was coming from on this. Where anyone might come from on it, actually. The *Daily Mail* would have a field day on a story like this. *Woman scams her way into Heartbreak Hotel and pretends to be long-lost (almost) stepdaughter.*

'Mum! You need to tell us how you know her. This is so flaming bizarre.'

As Nadia gestured with her free arm, she dislodged Flora's suction, who let out a squeal of indignation.

'I will. Feed Flora first. That's the most important thing.'

Nadia gave me a look as if to say, 'You can absolutely bet that I will be making my daughter a priority.' The 'unlike you' shimmered in a thought bubble above her head. I couldn't even begin to wrap my mind round the fact that two seismic events – Flora's birth and a reunion with Heather – had coincided. It was ironic, when most of the recent years had delivered nothing more noteworthy than an increasing difficulty in doing up my bra and a growing desire to complain about hot food served on cold plates.

Annie arrived with a jug of iced water and poured everyone a glass, then sat down, folding her hands into her lap and saying, 'Ronnie, I'm sorry. I shouldn't have blurted it out like that.' I gazed at this woman I'd known as Annie, the traces of little Heather in her face seeming so obvious now.

Before I could respond, Nadia's head snapped up. 'Why don't you let Mum have a drink, while you tell us how you came to be here? It sounds like an interesting story,' she said, arranging her face in the way TV detectives do when they have hardcore evidence that the suspect is lying. Marina had the hurt, huffy look of a long-time friend confronted with the fact that there was a part of my life that had been hidden from her. Her face carried the outrage of realisation that decades of friendship hadn't guaranteed the right to pick over every single bone in the skeleton of my history.

Annie's eyes sought my permission and I found myself wanting to control what was said. Instead, I nodded, feeling as though I was drifting out to sea with no clear plan on how to sail back to shore.

'I knew Ronnie from my childhood. I'll let her explain how. I was the sort of kid that everyone was always exasperated with, the "naughty one" that couldn't sit still. I was impulsive – still am – which often led to teachers not liking me, especially because I've never managed to go along with things that I didn't feel were fair, so I got into a lot of trouble for "talking back".'

She grinned at the memory. 'But when I met Ronnie, she realised that I had energy to burn. My sister and I spent a lot of our holidays in Cornwall, and she'd play with me for hours, teaching me to swim, jumping waves, diving for stones, doing acrobatics in the sea, which kept me out of mischief.'

I was touched that she remembered that, despite feeling that Annie was giving me credit for something deliberate. In reality, I loved the sea and, whereas most people I knew got bored after half an hour, Annie would keep me company until our fingertips shrivelled and our shoulders were pink from the sun.

I glanced at Nadia, weighing Annie's words, judging them against her own experience.

Nadia smoothed her face out. 'How old were you?'

Annie looked to me for confirmation. 'Four, I think, when we met, that first summer when you taught me to swim?'

My heart sank as the scales tipped against me. Matteo preferred the cool of the mountains to the beach in summer and Nadia had been quite old – eight, nine? – when she finally learnt to swim. She didn't like the water much even now.

'Where were your parents?' Nadia asked.

I watched Annie clear her expression like an old-fashioned Etch A Sketch. 'My mum was often away working; she was in a dance troupe. We lived in a flat in London, but my dad owned a house in Cornwall. My mother didn't like the countryside so she never joined us. We spent all our holidays there – Easter, summer and I think some Christmases. Some weekends too. My sister and I loved it. We had a tiny balcony in London and down there we had a garden and, of course, the beach.'

I waited for Nadia to put two and two together and, sure

enough, she drew her chin in, looking from Annie to me. 'And, let me guess, Mum was your "nanny"?'

I hated the way she said it, as though 'nanny' was synonymous with 'your dad's bit of fluff'. As though she expected no better. But I hadn't been any better. Not after that first summer anyway.

I tried to keep my voice light. 'Yes, I'd recently returned from a year in Paris, but there wasn't much call for interpreting and translating in Cornwall in 1971. We hadn't even joined the Common Market then. I needed to earn money and took the first job that I could find. I was terrified that Mum and Dad would come to rely on me at the farm and I'd never escape.'

Annie tilted her head, questioningly. 'You moved in to look after our house at some point, didn't you?'

I couldn't sit still. I stood up to pour myself more water, wondering how much Annie knew. 'Yes, your dad was keen for it not to stand empty and, after living in France, I was used to doing my own thing. I couldn't bear my parents asking where I was going and what time I'd be back, so I jumped at the chance.'

Nadia's face was a picture of disdain as she asked, 'And how long did you *work* for Annie's father?'

I wanted to draw back and dig my heels in, like Strega when we drew up outside the dog groomer's. 'Until 1976.'

Nadia frowned impatiently.

'Four and a half years,' I said.

'Four and a half years?!' She turned to Annie. 'You spent all your holidays with my mother? Didn't your own mother mind?'

Annie looked down. 'I'm not sure she really liked young children. She suffered with her nerves, or at least that's what they said back then. I now think she was depressed. She used to lie in bed a lot and, of course, I was a handful, so there was this underlying accusation that I made her worse.' She smiled in a way that masked a deep-seated hurt. Belatedly, she attempted to defend Nancy. 'She was quite a sought-after dancer in that period, so she was away a lot too.'

Thankfully, Flora chose that moment to throw up all over Nadia.

I jumped up. 'Oh dear. Do you want me to hold her while you go and get cleaned up? Actually, Flora probably needs a wipe-down too. I'll come in with you,' I said, relieved to have an excuse to make a start on damage limitation. Nadia didn't reply but didn't object to me following her out.

As soon as we set foot on the steps, Nadia said, 'You had an affair with her father, didn't you?'

'I didn't know he was still in a relationship with his wife. I thought he was getting divorced. I only ever saw him in Cornwall. He worked in London.' Even as I said the words, I wasn't sure whether this was the story I'd told myself so often over the years to lessen my guilt that it felt like the truth. Perhaps it was simply what I hoped was the reality, or maybe repeating it so regularly meant I could no longer recognise the lie.

'Come off it. The kids must have mentioned something about their parents being together. Eating baked beans on toast, watching TV, playing Cluedo. Something? Surely? You must have wondered where he was staying when he wasn't in Cornwall?'

I pushed open the front door. 'It was a long time ago. It wasn't like today when you can contact people on their mobile or see everything they are up to on social media. If we wanted to speak, he had to ring me on the landline. He was often abroad, and otherwise he was travelling up and down the country, selling wine to restaurants. I assumed he was staying in hotels. I took his word for it, accepted that sometimes he'd stay at the London flat to see the girls or that he needed to babysit or help out in some way. He'd told me his wife wouldn't agree to a divorce and, back then, you had to wait five years if that happened. I don't know, Nadia. I was young and—' I broke off.

No good would come from describing to my daughter that in the beginning I'd found him so mesmerising. I'd been so flattered when this grown-up, this mature man with houses and a career, appeared so fascinated by me. And how, later, when his car pulled up on a Friday night, I'd tried to ignore that jolt of distress as though I'd just realised I'd left my handbag on the platform as the train pulled out. How I denied my relief when he went out to the pub, leaving me with Heather and Lyndsey. How I listened for the garden gate grinding open so we could all scatter when he came back. How I didn't want to stay but didn't know how to leave without making sure the girls were in safe hands.

I could sense Nadia behind me, radiating accusation, as I let us into her apartment. I really was the gift that kept giving – no such thing as a normal relationship for me. It wasn't enough for her to have witnessed the toxic triangle of me, Matteo and Gianna. I'd now been outed as the flibbertigibbet, who'd played at being someone else's mother and had a dysfunctional love affair into the bargain. Annie's glowing reference of my abilities in loco parentis were unlikely to swing the pendulum back in my favour.

I braced for the machine-gun fire while I put the plug into the kitchen sink and ran the tap. Testing the warmth with my wrist, I lifted in Flora, gently scooping the water over her. Her eyes were beady and bright. The simplicity of babies. 'Look at you taking everything in. Sweetheart, you are,' I said, kissing her chubby fist. Without looking at Nadia, I said, 'If you give me a nappy and a vest, I'll get her dressed while you go and wash.'

Nadia hesitated, as though admitting that it would be easier to shower without Flora was akin to 'letting me win' or announcing a weakness to the world.

'Go on. She'll be fine.'

Nadia finally disappeared into the bathroom. I relaxed as I heard the water running. I dressed Flora and sat in an armchair, alternating between my disbelief at Heather reappearing and marvelling at the miracle of this tiny being. Those mini ears. The perfection of those eyelashes.

It was absurd that Marina and I had ever thought we could help other people remedy their relationships. If anything, I was the one desperately in need of assistance: to re-establish a bond that had been broken forty-seven years ago and to forge a new one with Flora. I hadn't even dared ask Nadia if she'd let Grant know he had a daughter. Selfishly, I wanted him to disappear forever, drop out of their lives, robbing him of the power to pull Nadia and Flora back to England. I dug deep for my conviction that it would be so much better for Flora to grow up with two parents, to have a proper connection to her dad. Unfortunately, when it came to my granddaughter, my wish to keep her close refused to be cowed by all that was right.

She yawned, an exaggerated, elongated oval. Having spent a good fifteen years looking at my friends' photos of their grandchildren and wondering how quickly I could move the conversation on, I now burned with the desire to photograph every breath, every nose wrinkle.

Nadia re-emerged in record time.

'Shall I take her for a little stroll in her pram? I'm happy to whizz her around the block,' I asked, trying to navigate a way back into Nadia's good books.

She shook her head as I knew she would. 'Thank you, but I'll sit up here with her in front of the fan. She can kick about next to me on the bed while I listen to a podcast.'

I wished that I could chip in and tell her about my favourite podcasts, impress on her that I was part of her world. I felt old. I could just about manage life on my mobile phone but still preferred a hard copy of a prescription, a train ticket, a newspaper. Nadia was always nagging me – 'You don't need to print it out! It's so wasteful.' I would have to get with it now. I didn't want Flora growing up seeing me as some antiquated fossil, stuck in the twentieth century, as alien to her as a fax machine.

I passed Flora over. 'I'll be downstairs.' I paused. 'I'm sorry that Annie's here at the moment and all this has blown up. I knew her as a little girl when I was in my twenties. It's not actually a big deal.' I needed to stop lying. It was *the* deal that defined my life. Big. Julia Roberts huge. However much I wished it wasn't.

Nadia pursed her lips. 'Make sure she doesn't ask you for any money. She definitely wants something from you, or she wouldn't be here.'

'My gut instinct is that she's a really genuine woman. My best guess is that she's trying to make sense of the past now her mother's died. Anyway, she's going home in a few weeks.'

Nadia was looking at me as though my naivety knew no bounds.

I turned to go, then took a big breath. 'In 1976, Annie – Heather, as she was then – her sister, Lyndsey, and their dad, Eddie, were in a car accident with me. Lyndsey was badly hurt but she recovered. Eddie was killed.' My throat went dry and I licked my lips, the words that I'd kept so tightly corralled inside me burning a passage into the wild.

Nadia's mouth flew open in shock. 'Mum! You were in an accident where someone died?'

I nodded and forced out the last bit of what I had to say. 'I was driving.'

Even after all these years, guilt clawed at my insides. The investigation had cleared me of dangerous driving, but for months afterwards, everywhere I went, conversations ground to a halt, as though someone had suddenly turned the volume down. Women adjusted their headscarves and pursed their lips, mothers pulled their children away from me and I'd hear my name skate across a hissed whisper. My years of 'living in sin' had come home to roost and there appeared to be plenty of people who considered I'd got my comeuppance and 'left two innocent young girls without a father'.

Nadia settled Flora on her shoulder. 'You killed someone in a car crash and you've never told us?'

I felt the blow of the truth I'd battled with, the responsibility that someone had died because I'd lost control of the car. And far, far worse than that was the knowledge that, in my darkest times, I'd even nurtured a fantasy that Eddie might die, freeing me and the girls from the exhausting rollercoaster of our awareness that his sunny moods would never last. From the knowledge that one day, but not which day, I would again be standing in front of Heather, shouting for her to run and lock herself in the bathroom.

Of course, the reality bore no relation to the relief of my daydreams. There was no release in Eddie dying, just grief at the way we'd lived.

I found my voice. 'The weather was terrible and I hit some black ice, then a van ploughed into us. The police said it could have happened to anyone. I wasn't convicted of anything.'

But Nadia was staring at me, horrified. 'What else have you been hiding all these years? Did Dad know about this? About Annie? And this Eddie bloke?'

I looked away, the sheer enormity of carrying such a burden for so long pressing down on me. I wanted to cry out that I was never allowed to see the girls again, not even to say goodbye and the sadness had nearly destroyed me. But it didn't seem the right moment to call attention to how much I'd loved someone else's daughters.

'They were different times, Nadia. People didn't talk about tragedies and feelings. We accepted that anything awful should be shoved into a concrete bunker and never discussed again.'

Nadia was shaking her head in disbelief. 'But it's so weird that you had this big thing happen to you and you were, what, pretty much a mother to two other girls and never thought to mention it?'

I walked towards the door before I met her anger with my own. I'm not sure what I expected. I'd obviously been hoping for a grain of compassion rather than a total focus on my 'selfishness' at keeping a secret. I hadn't spoken about it to anyone once I came to Italy. That's how things were then. In the end, I'd had to cauterise the wound in order to survive myself. My love for Heather and Lyndsey didn't count for anything. I was required to walk away from them, these little beings I'd sung to, rubbed noses with, taken to gather shells, *invested in*.

In the months that had followed that dreadful day, I'd walked the clifftops, always expecting to see Heather racing towards me, her wellies flapping, her hair flying. We'd often gone for a walk, the two of us, in all weathers, to get her out from under Eddie's feet. Lyndsey was easier, content to curl up with her Look-In annuals and dinosaur transfer books, a gentle breeze to Heather's whirlwind. I couldn't look at the towering bear's breeches, growing like triffids along the coastal paths, without remembering her bursting in with a bunch as tall as her for my birthday. I could never stand to hear the theme tune to *Happy Days* again; even a black leather jacket made my heart ache for the girls doing their incessant Fonzie impressions – 'Heee-yyyy' – until I begged them to stop.

I wasn't a parent, not even an official stepparent. And in the blink of an eye, it didn't matter that I'd spent nearly five years playing Mouse Trap or steeled myself to eat their home-made jam tarts without studying the grey pastry too closely. I'd earned no credits for sitting through countless 'shows' with Heather scolding Lyndsey for getting the dance steps to 'Tiger Feet' wrong and restarting the cassette.

For so long, I'd thought about them every day. I'd railed against the fact that a mother who'd been only too happy to pack off her children to Cornwall for the summer holidays while she high-kicked her way around the world, could snap her fingers and demand that we all stopped caring about each other. I'd had to accept my love for Heather and her sister would zigzag around the universe like a letter with an incorrect address, never reaching the recipient. And now Heather – Annie – was right here.

I shut the door behind me, saying, 'We can talk about this another day. I'll let you rest now,' when really I wanted to snatch mirrors off the walls and sweep vases from the shelves. Anything to relieve the fury inside me that somehow a horrible accident with such powerful consequences should become another stick to beat me with.

The need to lie down was so all-consuming that I went back to my own apartment and stretched out on my sofa, eager to drift into the blankness of sleep. But my mind whirred, desperate to understand whether my feelings for Heather and Lyndsey had 'finished' after a certain time of not seeing them or whether they had merely lain dormant. Had my emotions been in the deep freeze holding on for the day that this grown-woman version would appear, almost half a century later? What was in it for her? Curiosity? Answers? Did love die, especially if you weren't related? Would it be possible to pick up from the point where twenty-seven-year-old me was ripped away, with no warning, from eight-year-old her?

As if for good measure, my mind led me down other alleys it was unwise to go if self-preservation was my goal: whether Nadia would return to England, how she would survive without any support, how she would afford to live. I toyed with the idea of selling up in Rome and moving back to England myself. I dismissed that idea nearly as quickly as it presented itself. I'd been away too long. The last time I went back – four years ago, soon after Nadia married Grant – I'd felt a sense of dislocation. My instinctive understanding of how everything worked had disappeared. I'd been shouted at for standing on the wrong side of the escalator on the underground, tried to pay with an old five-pound note that was no longer legal tender, been too frightened to drive on the left-hand side of the road. That sense of belonging had vanished.

No. Going with her was not an option. I'd simply have to do everything I could to keep them here.

19

A tap at the door jolted me from my restless doze.

Annie.

'I hope I didn't wake you?'

'It's okay, I'm just taking a minute to rest. To absorb.'

'Can I get you anything?'

I beckoned her into the kitchen. 'I'll make some coffee.' I clattered about, my eyes heavy through lack of sleep, exacerbated by worry.

'I came to apologise and to ask if you want me to go back to England. I've made this all so difficult for you. I shouldn't have confronted Nadia like that. It was my clumsy attempt to say I've never forgotten what you did for me.'

I spooned coffee into the espresso maker. I didn't want to ask. I *had* to ask. 'What do you remember about your father?'

Her voice was quiet. 'I was frightened of him.'

The gas ignition clicked in the silence. I had no idea even at my age how much truth adult children could bear about their parents. Did it hurt less because we'd lived long enough to know that the people who brought us into the world, who should love us above everything, were imperfect beings?

'I was too,' I said.

I watched the pot spitting little splashes of coffee onto the hob. I was both repelled by and propelled towards what needed to be said out loud. It was as though we were about to open the door to a room long locked, with no idea whether we'd find it cobwebby but empty, or littered with a hundred skeletons in various stages of decomposition.

'Why did you stay with him?' she asked.

'Initially, love. Or what I mistook for love. There was a certain element of convenience to our relationship as well – he had a house and I felt impossibly grown up and decadent at twenty-three. I fancied myself as rather Parisian, cosmopolitan, trailblazing. Rather than a dairy farmer's daughter for whom the alternative would have been shovelling cow shit.' Annie didn't need to be burdened with the greedy sexual nature of our weekends when Eddie didn't have the children. When he arrived from London on a Friday night after I'd had all day to chill the champagne and drive to Looe to pick up ham and cheese straight from the farm before spending most of Saturday and Sunday in bed.

'I don't think my dad was very nice to you, was he?' Annie said, the words rolling out reluctantly, as though she was feeling her way across a bridge with rotting timbers.

I heated the milk. 'He could be very charming at times. It wasn't all bad. I did love the good bits about him.'

Annie stood up. 'Ronnie, I know what he did to you. You don't have to pretend to me.'

I poured the coffee, making cappuccinos for us both. 'Do you really want to do this? Do you want to hear it? Because I'm not sure you do. I'm not convinced anything positive comes from people adding clarification to bad memories. You obviously know he had a temper. I said that to you before I realised we were talking about your dad. I had hoped you wouldn't remember.'

'Lyndsey doesn't recall that at all. She won't have it. She's totally bought into Mum's "charismatic rogue, bit of a hothead" narrative.'

'Maybe that was her relationship with him, though? We don't interact with everyone the same – bits of our personality complement or clash with elements in other people's characters. Eddie didn't lose his temper with Lyndsey in the way he did with you. She was a different personality.' Despite myself, I smiled. 'She could conform. She could bend. You, my dear, always wanted to argue the toss, to be right. To make him see your point of view.' I tried to backtrack in case Annie might feel I was apportioning blame somehow. 'And that's one of your most amazing qualities. You were – still are – fearless. You don't back away from confrontation. You didn't even then. How he behaved with you was awful. He could be very cruel with his words if you didn't agree with him.'

And with his hands.

Annie chewed a nail. 'I think the minimum we should insist on from people around us is that they agree whether someone was a decent person or not. I do expect Lyndsey to have the balls to say she knows Eddie – Dad – could lash out. That how he behaved was wrong, that Mum was away with the fairies with her version of their "perfect' marriage. I could even bear it if Lyndsey said she loved Dad anyway because he treated her well, differently from me. But I can't stand this whole rewriting of history.'

I understood her need to have the people she loved validate her point of view. Nadia's refusal to condemn Matteo wholeheartedly for carrying on with Gianna for decades was a sore that kept on festering, ready to erupt whenever we crossed swords.

Just like she had when she was little, Annie was staring at me, directly, as though she trusted me to have a fair answer. I was getting to the age where I was a bit done with having to find the answers. Someone younger needed to figure them out now. I'd blunder on with my half-solutions, letting things ride.

I tried, feebly, for a cop-out. 'To be honest, you can waste a lot of time attempting to force people to see things as you do. I can't come up with a single instance when Nadia has snapped her fingers and said, "Do you know what, Mum? You're right, I got it all wrong." If anything, arguing my case has led to us becoming more entrenched. And I'm sorry to say, I don't think that's unique to me and my daughter.'

Annie flicked her hand in annoyance, as though she was disappointed I didn't have the backbone for a fight. She definitely wasn't yet ready to relinquish her right to the one and only truth.

In a move that reminded me a bit of Nadia when my response didn't concur with hers, she said, 'What I can't understand is when there was all that trouble at work, you know, when the owner's son became Dad's boss and he started drinking even more, why didn't you leave him?'

I couldn't weigh up all the various implications of saying what I really believed. I stirred my coffee to give me breathing space. The veracity of the words surprised me when I let them roll out unfiltered. I'd tried not to justify my behaviour, to make excuses for my cowardice in not walking away. 'I was planning to go, but the accident happened before I worked out what to do. I'd intended to find your mother in person, to tell her I understood how difficult things were with Eddie. I needed to persuade her to protect you two, and herself, from him somehow.' I looked down. 'I'd already tried to phone her, but that didn't go well, and there was a part of me that kept putting off confronting it all because I knew she wouldn't ever let me see you again. By that New Year, I was finally facing up to the fact that your father had probably never even asked for a divorce. It was always going to be an impossible conversation – the mistress turning up with suggestions on how she should deal with her husband and take care of her children.'

Annie sighed. 'She wouldn't have taken any notice of you anyway. I don't think she admitted to herself how bad it was. She'd have found a way to blame you for everything. Which is, in fact, what she did.'

'I should have left him earlier. I didn't do anyone any favours by holding on. For a long time, I fooled myself that it would get better when he was divorced, when we got married. I was deluded. But my love for you both was very real. I won't insult your mother by saying, "I loved you like my own children" because, back then, I was very critical of Nancy. I had no idea how hard it was to be a parent, that tremendous responsibility, the relentless questioning of your own judgement.' I shrugged at the simplicity of my thinking. 'All I concentrated on was having fun with you, which was the easy part. You were up for anything – swimming, surfing, rockpooling.'

Annie sipped her coffee. 'You were like a mother to me. I honestly think you were the only person who liked me when I was little. I felt wrong with everyone else – too clumsy, too loud, too tall. I made you laugh. I can't tell you how powerful that was. Me, the girl that everyone found annoying, making this cool woman with cut-off shorts and itsy bikinis throw her head back and erupt into giggles.' Her voice caught. 'I know I've been underhand, but it felt like serendipity when I saw that magazine article. I gave myself a fighting chance by sending you some liquorice. I remembered how you always asked me to buy liquorice laces when I went to the sweet shop in Fowey. Even if you hadn't chosen me for the apartment, I'd have come anyway. Probably just turned up on your doorstep. At least this way, I was able to work out whether the Ronnie of my memory was real or not.' Annie ran her fingers around the neck of her T-shirt. 'I wanted to talk about the other thing. That final thing.'

I found myself breathing out to ease the force of the memo-

ries this conversation was evoking, like horses released from a
burning stable, thundering wildly to freedom.

Annie lifted her head up, her eyes shining with tears. 'I
know the accident was my fault that day.'

I put up my hand. 'Don't. Don't say that. You were eight
years old. I was the one driving. I've thought about this so many
times. Maybe I've told myself something I can live with. It was
circumstances: the ice on that corner, the van speeding the
other way, your dad on the wrong end of too many ciders, losing
his temper and me trying to protect you.'

Tears were streaming down Annie's cheeks. 'I should have
stopped singing when he asked me.'

One of the glorious things about moving to Italy in 1978,
two years after the accident, was that I could bear to listen to
the radio again. I didn't constantly stumble over reminders of
Lyndsey, and Heather – as I still thought of her – doing their
Showaddywaddy dances or fighting over who was going to be
Kiki Dee and who would have to be Elton John.

'But you were eight. You sang everywhere. In the bath, in
bed, at the beach. You were doing what you always did. It was
your dad who suddenly decided he needed quiet and you
couldn't see the reason for it. You were a child who questioned
everything; you always had. It was a sign of intelligence, not
something that deserved a slap round the face. None of that was
your fault.'

'Do you really believe that? I've felt so guilty about it for so
long,' Annie said. 'Or are you just being kind?'

'I really believe it. More than believe it.'

Annie cried in that silent, shuddering manner that comes
from exorcising a hurt that's squeezed out of a deep place.

I put my arm around her. 'I'm the one who's been riddled
with what ifs – what if I'd never met your father, what if I
hadn't tried to interfere, what if I'd had more experience driving
his car, what if we'd decided to go for a walk instead of to the

pub... The variables were infinite, but they all collided in that one.'

'I never blamed you, Ronnie. Never. That's partly why I had such a difficult time with Mum. I used to stick up for you. Swearing that I'd caused the car accident that killed Eddie, not you.'

The idea of Annie's intense little face earnestly insisting on the facts made my chest fill with emotion. 'Thank you. That means a lot.' I gathered myself. 'But if I wasn't to blame, you definitely were not. Not at all. You can let go of any vestige of guilt about that. You and Lyndsey were the innocent ones in all of this.'

She swiped at her face. 'Sorry. I've longed to have this conversation. I've spent so much of my life feeling as though I'm mad, untrustworthy or that I'm somehow out of step with the way normal people function. I thought you were angry with me, because I never saw you again after that day.'

At that, I grabbed her hands. 'No. No. Not at all. My heart broke over that. I knew you'd think that. I wrote to you, to Lyndsey, to your mother. Begged her to let me see you both, just once, to say goodbye. To make it clear that I never blamed you. Not for a second.'

Annie said, 'I found your letter to my mother when I dealt with her paperwork. It was as though someone had collected all the jumbled fragments of my life and finally filed them in the right order. I'd had so many years of people presenting such a different version from how I remembered events that I almost convinced myself I was making it all up. I showed it to Lyndsey, but she didn't want to know. She said she had enough on her plate with Mum dying without digging up more trouble.'

As Annie spoke, I felt as though I was watching two different people side by side. One, a middle-aged woman with a compelling presence that made me want to lean forwards to follow the pattern of her thoughts – thoughts that darted about and demanded a certain mental agility to keep up. Alongside that, a determined child, the girl I recognised from years ago, impulsive and headstrong but who still glanced round to seek approval for something daring. Contrarily, if approval was granted, she would immediately lose interest.

'Was your coming out here to find me the straw that broke the camel's back with Lyndsey?'

'It didn't help matters,' she said, with a little grin.

'I've caused so much trouble in your life, yet here you are.'

She squeezed my fingers. 'No. No. That's not true. You were the only one who made me feel that I wasn't a bad person. I felt safe with you, as though you weren't suddenly going to whip round and list a hundred things that were wrong with me if I made a mistake or said something you didn't like.' Her voice grew louder as though she needed volume to convince me. 'I've clung onto that feeling. And because of you, I knew how to be with my sons. I wasn't – I'm not – a perfect mum, but whatever else I got wrong, they know they're loved and that they can always come to me whatever happens, however much they've messed up or failed.'

I couldn't speak, her words burrowing into the jagged place where regrets lay buried, bubbling and fermenting a little less ferociously as the years passed but never quite running out of oxygen. I had a sensation of pulling out everything I was ashamed of, everything I'd dreaded people discovering and throwing it down for all to see. And, alongside that, a mixture of relief and disbelief that this big thing I'd carried with me, this foetid and oozing tangle of wrongdoing writhing inside could be stilled, released into the wild to find a corner to curl up and die. The malevolent nucleus from which the rest of my life radiated was a collection of errors – wrong turns, misguided loyalty, mistaking passion for the proof of love. Nonetheless, it was still damning evidence that sometimes youthful folly can never be fixed, never reversed. Yet – with the balm of Annie's encouragement and forgiveness – the accident that had robbed her of her father seemed like an injury that could finally heal, albeit knottily and imperfectly, rather than a live sore still able to infect the future.

I hugged Annie, pressing my face into her shoulder, marvelling at the physical ease between us that I'd always lacked with Nadia as an adult. 'I'm glad you found me,' I whispered. Then I said it again, loudly, defiantly.

'I'm sorry my timing wasn't better. Talk about emotional overload for you. Me, Nadia turning up, a new grandchild.'

'Give me time to square things with her. Our history' – I gestured to us both – 'has had a knock-on effect. I never managed to love freely again. Not on purpose, of course. But I missed you both so terribly for so long. I thought having my own daughter would somehow mitigate that, but it made me think about you more, if that was possible. I hated the idea that you would feel abandoned, that you would assume I didn't care. It was all so traumatic, I was desperate to know you were okay but there was no way of finding out anything. None at all. I even rang your mother a couple of times, but you can imagine how well that went. Not that I blame her. Eventually, I decided that you'd be better off without me, and for my own sanity, I was forced to accept that you were only meant to be in my life for a season. To be honest, I'm amazed that you even remembered me.'

Annie leaned back, her expression earnest. 'I never forgot you. I'd like to think I can be part of your life again.'

'Me too,' I said, my stomach already fizzing with worry at Nadia's reaction.

I didn't want to be forced to choose between them.

20

Over the next few days, I snatched time with Annie, my delight at our reunion clashing against Nadia's stabbing disapproval. My ease with Annie held up an unflattering mirror to my relationship with my daughter, reflecting our resentments, our missteps, our inability to communicate off every surface.

I tried to talk to Nadia, but she kept closing the conversation down, saying, 'You obviously had your reasons for keeping your secrets' in a tone that suggested whatever my reasons were, they had absolutely no value as far as she was concerned. It took me all my willpower not to say 'Pot, kettle, black' and rake up the Gianna and Matteo debacle again.

Added into the mix was Marina, who was struggling to work out her own reaction to the fact that I'd kept a chunk of my past under wraps for our entire friendship. She vacillated between grudging admiration – 'And there was me thinking you were an open book and instead little Ronnina had a thumping great secret all these years' – and outrageous off-colour comments that left me gasping in horror – 'I've no idea why you've spent all your life doing some ridiculous hair shirt self-flagellating thing. From what I've learnt about Eddie, you did the world a favour killing him off like that.' A couple of times, she dropped her cantankerous dowager act and said sadly, 'I wish you'd told me. I thought you trusted me.'

'I did. I do. When I first came to Rome, it was too painful to think about. I'd cut my ties with England, with my own family. I needed you to replace them. I was frightened of telling you something that would make you back away or like me less. I was afraid to risk our friendship. I couldn't have survived without you.' Marina and I never spoke like this. We never acknowledged how much we needed each other, disguising our reciprocal love with the barbed banter that underpinned an unspoken promise to have each other's back, no matter what the circumstance.

Marina looked both surprised and mollified. 'Well, most of my other friends are dead or demented, so I suppose I'll have to forgive you. Still, you are a dark horse. I shall await future revelations with great anticipation.'

'You know everything there is to know now.'

Marina harrumphed and resumed her critical manner as though she'd pressed pause by accident. 'If you want to stand half a chance of seeing Flora grow up, you'd better worry a bit less about forging a relationship with a girl you knew decades ago and pull out all the stops with Nadia. I heard her on the terrace chatting to Grant first thing. Couldn't quite grasp all of the conversation – I leaned over my balcony as far as I dared, but I was afraid I might end up on the tarmac.'

'How can you be certain it was Grant she was talking to?' I wasn't even aware that Nadia had told him about Flora's birth. But then, I was often the last to know anything. No change there.

'She sounds much softer when she's speaking to him. Much more gentle, less bulldozerish.'

'Does she? I hadn't noticed.' I allowed myself a little smirk at the idea that Marina – bulldozer extraordinaire – was passing judgement on the trait in someone else.

Though now Marina mentioned it, Nadia did consider Grant's opinions far more than she ever took notice of anyone else's views. But maybe that was love. Perhaps even the most stubborn people found it within themselves to compromise if the stakes were high enough. Thank goodness that getting rid of her baby had been a concession too far.

'So did you get the gist of what she was saying?' I had a half-second attack of conscience that I shouldn't encourage Marina to snoop before my determination to be forewarned and fore-armed triumphed.

'At one point I think she was trying to get Grant to come here. Then I couldn't make out if she was saying she might return to England when Flora was old enough.' Marina tutted. 'I used to be able to hear what was being said when people had their backs turned on the other side of a room. It was one of my skills – catching people out who weren't even talking to me. Bloody old age.'

Marina's words made me want to bang on Nadia's door to plead with her not to take Flora away. 'When she said she might go back to England, do you think she meant for a visit? Or permanently?'

Marina screwed up her face with the effort of recalling the conversation. 'She definitely said something about missing him and England and wanting to take Flora to Cornwall.'

'Cornwall? I don't think she's ever been there.' I clutched at straws. 'I can't see a city girl like Nadia settling in a rural community. She must have meant a holiday. Maybe hearing about my past has piqued her curiosity and she'd like to see where I grew up,' I said, attempting to convince myself that there was no danger of her leaving permanently.

I wasn't sure if hearts became less able to withstand life's blows as we got older, but I had no intention of putting mine to the test. The thought of Nadia cupping that little head and disappearing to the airport in a taxi caused me physical pain.

I told myself off for being selfish, that a mother's lot was to swallow down her own heartache and rejoice that her child was happy. Of course I would support Nadia in whatever was right for her and Flora. I would. That was my job. But it would still be so much better if Nadia got rid of that self-righteous pedant and stayed exactly where she was. Though, if push came to shove, I could teach myself to tolerate Grant if he came to live here.

When I articulated that out loud to Marina, she drew herself up to her full height, leaned in and said, 'Get a grip. The last thing we need in this apartment block is a man with more opinions than me.' She did a naughty impression of Grant. '*Person-lleeee, I think anyone who needs a glass of wine with their dinner every day has a problem with alcohol.*' She shuddered. 'Just thinking about it makes me want to pop the cork on a bottle of Prosecco. In fact, I'm going to have a glass now.'

'It's only twelve o'clock.'

'Stop being so English. You're as bad as he is,' she said, banging her stick on the flagstones in irritated defiance.

I waved her off. 'Go and drink yourself into a stupor under the olive tree. Is that better?'

'Yes,' Marina said, stamping away with an ostentatious wobble of her buttocks.

I tiptoed along the corridor to reassure myself that Nadia wasn't already in the middle of packing. Flora's exhausted cries were echoing through the door. I knocked, despite a racing certainty that my intrusion wouldn't be welcome.

She appeared in her pyjamas with Flora in a sling, her little fists balled in protest. I forced myself to keep my attention on Nadia. 'I just wondered if you wanted to come over for lunch. Or I can bring some food to you. Or take Flora while you get dressed?' *Or anything that means you'll stay here forever and let me be part of my granddaughter's life.*

Nadia looked at me with eyes that didn't seem to focus. 'I'm not hungry.'

'You need to keep your energy up.'

Nadia's face clouded. 'I know.'

I tried again. 'This bit of motherhood is so hard,' I said as Flora's body went rigid in an effort to produce more noise than a tiny being should be capable of. 'It does get easier, I promise, but it is horrible feeling so worn out all the time.'

'I'll live,' Nadia said over Flora's yells.

I kept my voice steady. 'Why don't you sort yourself out while I walk her around the garden?'

Nadia nodded, but still managed to give me the impression she was reluctant to hand Flora over.

Between us, we prised the hot bundle of fury out of the sling and into my arms. 'Go on. She's fine. I can cope.'

With a weary slump of her shoulders, Nadia said, 'Thanks. I won't be long. Keep her in the shade, won't you? And don't leave her with Annie, will you?'

'No, of course not. Don't worry.' I wanted to argue that Annie was far more up to date on how to look after a baby than I was, never mind a genuine and kind-hearted person. Instead, I kept my counsel and jiggled Flora gently, shushing her and marvelling at the difference between how tolerant I felt towards Flora compared with the irritation I remembered when Nadia cried as a baby. I'd just wanted her to stop wailing and sleep so I could get on with – what? What was it that was so urgent? What made me feel that any time spent rocking Nadia to sleep or patting her back to bring up wind was precious time away from the other things I needed to be doing? Right now, I couldn't imagine anything I'd *rather* be doing than soothing Flora, reassuring her with the circles of my fingertips on her back that the world was a safe place and that she would know so much love. Perhaps age provided that patience, the knowledge that nothing lasts forever, that all phases – crying babies, unfaithful husbands, annoying friends – pass eventually or cease to matter. Or maybe I'd reached a stage when I didn't need to take so much from life, when I could give without worrying about what I was missing out on. That hurry, that frenetic focusing forwards but still glancing backwards, to see if I'd accidentally swept past something better than whatever I was doing in that moment had left me. Thank goodness I'd lived long enough for the privilege of appreciating the here and now.

The heat of July hit us as we emerged into the light, Strega trotting in our wake. Flora frowned at me as I carried her down the steps, a ladder of little wrinkles furrowing her forehead, followed by one last burst of loud rebellion. Then, like a window blind rolling up to reveal an unexpectedly sunny day, her face smoothed out. Her lips quivered and pursed as though she'd suddenly realised they could form more than one shape and didn't have to stretch open in a wide-mouthed yell.

'There. That's not so bad, is it?'

We moved into the shade of the garden. With an effort, I squatted down to show her my geraniums. Despite having brought up my own daughter, I was still pretty ignorant about what patterns or colours a ten-day-old baby could see. No doubt Grant would have been able to fill me in with parallelogram, hexagon and trapezium detail across the whole Pantone spectrum.

I had to stop maligning Grant, even if it was mainly within the confines of my mind. It would be better for Flora if she had a dad in the picture. *But not as good as having a grandmother with time and love to spare on hand every day of your life*, argued the little voice in my head.

I turned as the gate clicked open.

Annie came in. 'Am I interrupting?'

'Not at all. Nadia's busy getting herself together. I think she's worn out.'

'No one prepares you for how hard it really is. Everyone jokes about lack of sleep once you have a baby, but I told myself if it was that bad, people wouldn't do it. God had a good laugh at that. With Dylan, my firstborn, I used to cry in the shower every morning to get it over with for the day.'

I laughed. 'An effective use of time at least, doing two things at once. I clearly remember thinking that I'd never feel normal again. And then, one day, you suddenly realise that you feel fine but you can't pinpoint when everything changed.'

The way Annie sank down onto the grass drew my attention. There was a heaviness about her, a sadness enveloping her.

I pulled over a chair and settled Flora in my lap. 'Are you okay?' I asked.

'Yes, I'm fine.'

I leaned back, letting the sounds of Rome wash over me – the vans hammering down the hill outside, the distant hooting of horns, and here, close to home, the tiny clicks of Flora's tongue and Strega's snuffling. Without looking at Annie, I said, 'Have you been in touch with your sister? Does she know that we've connected again?'

'Yes. I left her a message.'

I sat up. 'And?'

'It wasn't quite the response I'd hoped for.'

I didn't know what to say to that. A wave of tiredness rolled over me that events from nearly half a century ago still had the ability to destabilise my life and those around me.

'I'm sorry to hear that. I don't suppose there's anything I can do to help?' I stroked Flora's chubby leg, comforted by the feel of her soft skin, the glorious, unspoilt newness of her.

'I wish there was. She feels I made a sport out of baiting my mother when she was alive by not buying into her guff about how her "heart and soul died the day Eddie died".'

'And I guess you're too polite to tell me that Lyndsey hates me for the role I played in it all – by being involved with your dad in the first place and then, well, the accident.'

The truth winced on Annie's face before she could disguise it. 'She's choosing what she decides to remember, or, at least, what she decides to fixate on.'

Flora wriggled and I traced a little pattern on her stomach. 'I don't think that's unique to Lyndsey.'

Annie got up. 'I'm going out for a walk. I need to clear my head.'

'If you can wait for a few minutes while I take Flora upstairs, I'll come with you. There's something I'd like to show you.'

Annie's face brightened. 'Great. I'm fidgety, though. Are you happy for me to scrub the patio in the meantime?'

'It's a bit hot for that, but be my guest.'

Upstairs, I pushed Nadia's door open. She was dressed, but with her hair off her face, wrapped in a towel, she looked absolutely exhausted.

I faltered for a moment, feeling guilty about disappearing with Annie. 'I thought I'd pop out for a bit unless you want to sleep?'

Nadia reached for her daughter, the reflex of putting Flora above her own needs already automatic. She kissed her head. 'Are you going out with Annie?'

I couldn't quite meet her eye. 'She's only got a few weeks left; I didn't want her to miss the Diavù portraits.' I forced myself to look at Nadia, aware that we never explored Rome together. 'I'm happy to go another day, if you need me?'

'You get on really well with her, don't you?' Nadia said, shifting Flora onto her shoulder.

'We had a lot of intense history together. Her dad was a troubled man.'

Nadia put her head on one side. 'How do you mean, troubled?'

I still found it hard to speak about, as though I was the one who'd caused Eddie's behaviour. Shame was still my automatic reaction, my go-to response, despite knowing, logically, that no one deserved to take the brunt of someone else's temper.

'He was violent and I stayed with him for much longer than I wanted to in order to keep the girls safe.'

Nadia gasped and instinctively cradled Flora's head with her hand. 'Did he hit you?'

I nodded.

Nadia blinked rapidly as she processed my words. 'That must have been awful. You poor thing. Did you tell your parents?'

'I didn't tell anyone. Looking back, I don't even know why. Pride, maybe. Not wanting them to say, "I told you so." At the time, I thought I could handle it, or somehow behave differently to make it stop. And there were lovely times in between...' I trailed off.

Nadia's expression was one of horror that I'd even contemplated accepting moments of joy from a man like that.

I waved the words away. 'I'm not sure I can explain it even now. It's complicated.'

Nadia burst out with, 'Well, it doesn't sound complicated to me. He sounds awful, Mum. You should have reported him to the police.'

'They wouldn't have taken me seriously, Nadia. Domestic violence wasn't recognised. There wasn't even any legislation against it until 1976. Ironically, the law was passed a few months after Eddie died.'

Shock flared across Nadia's face. 'You dealt with all that, and the accident, on your own?'

'More or less. That's how it was at the time. We just got on with things.'

'Did you have any counselling?'

I suppressed a snort. 'No one had counselling, or at least, not anyone I knew. I don't think it even existed then. Well, certainly not for people like us. Once the police investigation into the accident was over and they'd decided I wasn't at fault, I don't think my parents ever referred to it. Or the girls. As far as they were concerned, they weren't my children so it didn't matter that I never saw them again. I didn't have the words to tell anyone how I felt. That's why I came to Rome a couple of years later. I couldn't stand all those memories flaring up every time I went anywhere.'

Nadia laid Flora down in the Moses basket. She swiped at her eyes and put her arms around me. 'Bless you, Mum.'

As I walked back down to the garden, I felt the imprint of her body, the softness of her post-partum stomach, the tenderness of her touch. And despite everything, I was smiling.

21

Annie looked at me quizzically as I came down the steps, but perhaps sensing my lightness of spirit, she didn't intrude on my privacy. She hopped up behind me on the Vespa, quite the professional pillion passenger by now, clinging on with the lightest of touches and only screaming occasionally.

I headed to the outskirts of Trastevere and parked at the bottom of a flight of steps.

'Wow,' Annie said, looking up at the picture of a woman in a huge bonnet painted across the wide expanse of the stairs. 'That's beautiful.'

'It's by an artist called Diavù. He paints icons of the Italian cinema on flights of stairs – this is Elena Sofia Ricci, but he's also done Ingrid Bergman, Michèle Mercier and Anna Magnani. He's so clever because he paints on the rise, not on the tread. Can you imagine how smart you have to be to design something this big that has to work on stairs, not even on the flat?'

I looked towards the top. My knees sagged at the thought. It had to be done.

'Right. Follow me.'

I started to climb, gritting my teeth against the ache in my joints. I lost count after forty steps and was delighted to grind to a halt on the upper edge of Elena's bonnet so I could stop holding my breath to avoid grunting with the effort. I dabbed at my face with the back of my hands. Nadia would be so annoyed if she could see me sweating uphill in the midday sun.

'Look down. What can you see of the painting?'

Annie looked puzzled. 'Is this a trick question?'

'No. Just tell me exactly what's in front of you.'

She stuck out her bottom lip. 'A thin line of paint on the far edge of every tread.'

'So can you tell what the painting is from here?'

She shook her head.

'And what could you see when we were standing on the pavement?'

'The whole thing – her face, her hair, her hat.' She opened her palms in a questioning motion of 'where are we going with this weird conversation?'

'So it's fair to say that you can only see the complete picture when you are in the right position, as Diavù intended, looking from the pavement?'

She nodded, her expression mottled with a cloud of suspicion that seventy-four years had honeycombed the bit of my brain that governed sensible conversation. Bless Annie, though, her English reserve won out and she played along instead of launching into a dramatic hand gesture of 'Have you lost your mind?' as Marina would have done.

'Good.' I sank down onto the steps, wanting a minute to consider how to define the purpose of this outing.

'Are you okay?' Annie asked, crouching down.

'Yes, a bit hot.' I patted the concrete next to me.

We sat in silence for a moment, watching a couple of teenagers kiss as though they were alone in the world. Annie smiled. 'Wouldn't it be lovely to be that young again?'

I leaned against the ridge of the step, feeling it press into my spine. 'No, I like the age I am now. I've learnt to live with other people's disapproval without feeling that I have to change. I was trapped in this constant battle when I was younger, wanting to belong, wanting to please people, yet not managing to behave in a way so that I could. Now I don't care about fitting in as long as I've been decent, honest and fair.'

'I can totally relate to that. Maybe that's why I took to you so strongly when I was a child. I did feel that I fitted with you.'

I reached for her hand. 'As wonderful as it is to see you again after so long, I'm now riddled with fear that the more you know about me, the more you'll be disappointed in me.'

Annie nudged me gently. 'Don't be silly. You're one of the coolest people I know.' She ran her fingers through the hair on the nape of her neck. 'I'm not sure my pale skin is going to be able to withstand this direct sun for much longer.'

'Okay, let's go. But do you want to know why I brought you here?' I asked, as we made our way down.

'I've no doubt there is a method in your madness.'

'These Diavù paintings remind me of you and your sister. You're both seeing each other's point of view from the top of the bonnet, so you can only glimpse tiny fragments, a little strip here and there that makes sense. Whereas if you moved yourself around, you'd be able to take in the whole panorama.'

Annie almost shouted at me. 'But none of what Lyndsey says makes sense. My mother and father weren't happily married, he was often bad-tempered and sometimes downright scary and violent – you know that. And my mother was a hopeless fantasist who couldn't be bothered with young children and was far more attracted to swanning round the world with her dance troupe.'

'That's what you see. But if you swapped places with Lyndsey, if you stood at the foot of her steps, how would it look different?'

'I get your point,' she said, 'but it feels as though she's making my agreeing with her version of the past a condition of us having a relationship.'

'You were close up until your mother died, weren't you? And from what you've said, you weren't agreeing with Lyndsey before then, yet you still managed to rub along.'

'While Mum was alive, it was as though Lyndsey thought there was still time for me to buy into Mum's narrative and now that possibility has disappeared, she finds it disrespectful to her memory that I won't accept it.' Annie was waving her arms about in frustration, in a gesture so Italian that it made me smile inwardly.

'And, presumably, you finding me pushes you even further away from her version of events?'

Annie nodded.

I reached the pavement at the bottom. 'What if you conceded that the way she remembers things was how it was for her? Now both your parents are dead, does it really matter? Do you have to force her to admit you are right? What if you acknowledged that because you have dissimilar personalities, you interacted differently with your parents, so what might be true for her wasn't the same for you?'

Annie puffed her cheeks out. 'But what about when she harps on about Mum and Dad?'

'Assuming she has other topics of conversation if you manage to navigate this fallout, how much time do you think she'll talk about them? Five per cent of the time, ten? Could you concentrate on the ninety per cent that will be interesting and sing a song in your head for the other ten? Kind of disconnect so what she says doesn't rile you so much?'

Annie adopted that belligerent expression that people display when they are wedded to dying in a dramatic and theatrical manner on their chosen hill.

I walked over to the Vespa and handed her a helmet. 'Think about it.'

When we arrived back at the palazzo, Flora's wails drifted down from Nadia's apartment.

Annie said, 'Poor Nadia. I wonder if Flora's got colic.'

'I should probably go up.' I itched to have a crack at soothing her, at working what I secretly imagined to be my special grandma magic.

Annie put her hand on my forearm. 'Thank you for taking me to see the Diavù steps. I know you've got my best interests at heart but—'

I interrupted her. 'No need to explain. If I had all of life's answers, I wouldn't be second-guessing myself, wondering whether Nadia would appreciate some help or want me to keep my nose out. It's always so much easier to find the solutions to everyone else's problems rather than your own.'

Annie followed me up and I rapped on Nadia's door.

'Is everything okay?' I asked, almost conspiratorially, hoping her compassion from earlier had signalled the start of a kinder, more understanding approach between us.

'Why shouldn't it be?' she replied.

I sighed. Clearly that was a momentary lull and we were back to confrontational business as usual, though I got the distinct impression that Annie's presence was exacerbating the situation.

'No reason, love, except that your body's still battered and bruised and it takes time to adapt to being responsible for another little human.'

'I've got to suck it up, haven't I? It's not like I've got a husband to help.' She frowned at Annie.

The volume from Flora inside was increasing. Every cell in my body wanted to rush to her, but I didn't know how to break through whatever it was stopping Nadia letting someone else take the strain for an hour or two.

Annie spoke up. 'Please let us help. You don't have to do this all on your own.'

My shoulders flew up around my ears as I braced myself for Nadia telling Annie to keep her beak out, but instead she crumpled into tears. 'I don't know what's wrong with her. I keep thinking she's hungry, but she doesn't seem interested in feeding. She won't stop screaming. I can't put her down and the whole place is such a tip. Maybe my milk is rubbish. Perhaps she'd be happier on a bottle.'

Nadia had shouted at me when I'd suggested she might buy some formula to keep in reserve 'just in case', so this was a definite turn-up for the books. I didn't dare open my mouth for fear of being shot down in flames.

Annie seemed much more confident. 'Sometimes babies don't even know why they're screaming. Let me give you a hand to have a quick tidy-up. Perhaps your mum can give Flora a cuddle.'

I pushed down the little bubble of incredulity that Nadia wasn't bellowing at Annie to butt out but rather stood back to allow us in. She headed over to the Moses basket, where Flora was doing a great impression of a furious raspberry. Through sobs, Nadia said, 'Am I doing something wrong? Do you think she sensed that Grant and I didn't really want her? In the beginning, anyway? I mean, I do now, of course, but I'm not very good at motherhood.'

Annie pulled Nadia into a hug and although Nadia didn't exactly fold into her, she did rest her head on Annie's shoulder and permit herself a howl of unhappiness.

I gathered my courage to speak. 'Naddy. You're doing a brilliant job. You love Flora now she's here and that's all that matters. Can I pick her up?'

Nadia managed a muffled yes and I swooped in like a pig

rewarded for its perseverance with a prize-winning truffle. I tried not to dwell on the particular dynamic in my family that made the simple act of holding my granddaughter to comfort her yet another thing to use as a bargaining chip. How did other families sail along, pitching unasked into the harbour at exactly the right moment without all this plodding through permissions and weighing up of words?

I cuddled Flora and kissed her hot face, humming 'Twinkle, Twinkle, Little Star'. I surreptitiously watched Annie set to work, stacking up all the clean things from the dishwasher and reloading it, while Nadia swept the floor. Despite all the many previous sparks of hope that had fizzled out, I still experienced a burst of optimism that this time could be the turning point.

I found myself singing 'Give Me Joy in My Heart' very quietly to Flora – a hymn I hadn't sung since I went to church with my parents as a teenager. Even though I complained about the Sunday service, there was a certain comfort in standing next to my dad, his bulky farmer's frame tamed into a suit, the force of a voice trained to shout over tractors ringing up into the rafters in a capable baritone. How carelessly I'd thrown that relationship away, prioritising my need to be right. I'd been determined that my own anguish was far more significant than anything they were experiencing. My desire to punish them for not being the parents I wanted in that moment obscured every possibility of a satisfying connection going forwards.

Seventy-four was a bit late to realise that no one ever argued their way to happiness. I'd never properly understand why Nadia didn't tell me Matteo was having an affair, but at this point, did understanding even matter? I kissed the top of Flora's head and gave myself over to the calmness of believing that although Nadia's behaviour had hurt me, there hadn't been a malicious intention behind it.

I hoped one day she'd understand that I hadn't kept my own secrets to hurt her but to protect myself.

22

Over the next couple of weeks, the atmosphere in our palazzo loosened, the tension between all of us giving way to something more forgiving, less judgemental. In true Italian style, we took Flora to our local restaurant one evening, where the owner greeted us like royalty, fussing over Nadia and Flora and bowling over with a bottle of Prosecco on the house in celebration. I didn't even pretend not to be the proudest grandmother in the history of the world.

When Flora started to scream before Nadia had finished her risotto al radicchio, the owner's wife, Cinzia, appeared with a brand-new pacifier on a plate. I had a disloyal but nearly irresistible temptation to whip out my phone and film the horror on Nadia's face. A courteous but firm exchange of views followed, which ended with Cinzia shrugging her shoulders and disappearing with the offending item.

Annie was shaking her head in wonder. As she said, 'I've seen it all now,' Cinzia returned and, with the most cursory request for permission, whisked Flora out of Nadia's arms and waltzed off around the restaurant. She danced with her in front of the mirror, with every waitress pausing with armfuls of gnocchi and creamy tagliatelle to coo over her. Cinzia showed her to a table of priests who were knocking back red wine in a way that made me think the morning mass might be a challenge. I was waiting for Nadia to scoot after her and demand the return of her baby, but Cinzia's manner – honed by helping her three daughters bring up a whole army of grandchildren – obviously inspired confidence.

Annie couldn't get over our welcome. 'We took my oldest boy, Dylan, to a posh organic restaurant when he was about five months old and my husband and I were still labouring under the illusion that a baby wasn't going to change anything. We spent the whole lunchtime taking it in turns to walk up and down outside with him while the owner huffed and puffed and muttered about how children didn't belong in restaurants.'

Nadia said, 'Italy is a great place to bring up kids,' and I wanted to cover Cinzia in kisses as she handed over Flora and proclaimed her 'una gioia'. Flora had certainly tripled the joy in my life.

Even Marina managed to get on a semi-right page for once and said, 'English people love dogs far more than they love children. The last time I went to that place – what do you call it, where all the posh polo clubs are? Yes, the Cotswolds with...' She put a finger to her lips and then did one of her secret smirks as though she'd remembered that whoever she'd gone with should never become common knowledge. 'Anyway, never mind, the dogs were sprawling all over the floor with everyone having to step over them, their owners feeding them from their plates and letting them climb up on the chairs. Every silly yappy thing was getting into fights with other dogs and the landlords still brought out special snacks for them. No one batted an eyelid. The minute a child screamed or threw a tantrum, the whole pub was sucking in its cheeks.'

'That's not true, Marina,' Nadia said. 'Well, the dog bit is, but lots of places are child-friendly now.'

Marina did her haughty face. 'If you mean you can find those things – what are they called, the chicken nuggets – pah, not even chicken, just dirty crumbs swept off the floor – everywhere, then I suppose it is child-friendly.'

It would have been a waste of breath trying to persuade Marina otherwise, so I moved her on from the damning indictment of my country of birth by asking for the pudding menu. However, a tiny part of me was applauding Marina's contribution to discouraging Nadia's return to England.

While Annie and I deliberated over an *affogato* or *torta della nonna*, Marina asked Nadia if she'd heard from her 'no-good husband'. I stiffened with the fear of our convivial evening souring. I was, however, also talking loudly about how wonderful a scoop of vanilla ice cream in hot coffee was while stretching my ear out like a cartoon cat around a corner to hear the answer.

Nadia batted her hand at Marina. 'Don't call Grant that. He's still Flora's dad.'

A stream of Italian followed, of which the basic gist was the irony of men providing sperm and refusing to accept the consequences of the resulting pregnancy, yet having the gall to expect the deciding vote on what a woman does with her body. It was an odd universe in which Marina sounded like more of a feminist than Nadia. She finished with a flourish. 'Presumably you've told Grant to get lost and never be found again? Flora doesn't need a man like that in her life.'

A level of pain passed over Nadia's face and although I knew she wouldn't want me interfering, I snapped my fingers at Marina. 'Enough with the inquisition. Let the poor girl relax without you haranguing her.' Too late I remembered that Nadia hated being referred to as a girl, but she let it go.

Annie joined me in dragging the evening back on track, asking Nadia about her work and whether she missed it. Luckily, Cinzia arrived with mini bottles of limoncello, which immediately claimed Marina's focus.

After our mainly successful evening at the taverna, Nadia grew more confident about leaving the house, taking Flora in her stroller for a walk. Occasionally, she invited me to go with her and I always chose the route past the row of neighbourhood shops. I paraded Flora in front of the greengrocer's, the *tabacchi*, the florist's, waving to all the shopkeepers in the hope that they'd come out and fawn over her. I barely recognised myself, but at the same time, I was rather taken with this unrestrained loving-without-limits version of me.

Slowly, I also noticed a burgeoning friendship between my daughter and Annie, with Nadia thrusting out clumsy olive branches, which Annie, to her credit, accepted graciously: 'Do you want to walk up to the Vatican with me? Only because it's beautiful. I don't believe in organised religion.' I had no doubt that when the time came, Nadia would justify Flora playing with dolls as a necessary exercise in developing empathy and increasing her social skills, rather than anything as unsophisticated as 'just having fun'.

Nevertheless, my heart soared and sang to see the three of them in the garden, Annie drip-feeding maternal wisdom in a way that Nadia could absorb. My petty soul occasionally bristled as Nadia greeted Annie's suggestions as moments of epiphany, when I'd said exactly the same thing two weeks ago to bursts of derision. However, with my new mantra of not needing to be right, I chased away those sparks of annoyance. Instead, I concentrated on the relief that I didn't have to confront the conundrum of adoring another mother's daughter at the expense of my own flesh and blood.

Flora was flourishing, though Nadia could still be as spiky as a sea urchin if I dared to offer any advice. I'd once been bold enough to query whether Flora needed to be on the breast quite so often. Nadia had blowtorched my 'old-fashioned notions that there should be a fixed time between feeds' with enough force to take a plane out of the sky, so subsequently I clenched my teeth together whenever I felt inclined to comment.

I'd had Federico's son, Renzo, set up some shady sails across the garden so that Nadia could leave Flora to sleep outside without worrying. After baulking at the expense for so many years, I wished I'd done it sooner. And so did Marina. 'It's like we've built an extension that we can use all year round. We made a good decision there.'

I had a little smile to myself that Marina's contribution to our newfound outdoor freedom amounted to encouraging me to phone Renzo, but I was discovering the liberation of letting things go.

After the initial chaos that newborn babies bring, the whole palazzo had found a fresh rhythm. I often stumbled across Annie and Nadia in the garden first thing in the morning, with Flora kicking on a sheet. Nadia enjoyed flexing her intellect against Annie's sharp brain, engaging in heated debates about climate change, education, the NHS without descending into acrimony.

This morning as I wandered in with a tray of coffee, they both fell abruptly silent.

'Have I interrupted something?'

'No, no, not at all,' Annie said. 'I was telling Nadia how being here has made me a bit more open to seeing things from my sister's point of view.'

I clapped my hands together. 'I'm delighted to hear that,' I said, guilty that I'd been so focused on Nadia that Annie's troubles with Lyndsey had dropped down my priority list.

'I'm going to invite her to Cornwall for a weekend when I get back, the two of us, see if she'll walk some familiar paths with me and hopefully put to bed a few memories.'

I shivered. 'That's brave. Are you sure that's the way to go?'

Annie nodded. 'That's the plan, but she's got to agree to spending a few days with me first.'

'July is flying by so quickly. You're leaving us in a little over four weeks, aren't you?' A rush of sadness engulfed me as I reflected on how quickly I'd become used to Annie's company, how much there was still to catch up on.

A glance passed between Nadia and Annie.

'What?'

Nadia bit her lip. 'I've decided to travel back to England with Annie when she leaves in the last week of August. I've already applied for a passport for Flora.'

I couldn't help it; I gasped. 'Whatever for? Flora will only be a couple of months old. She's very young to take on holiday.'

Annie gave it away, by how she uncurled her fingers in readiness to put a soothing hand on my arm.

My heart felt the blow before my brain caught up. 'It's not a visit, is it? Are you moving back there?'

Nadia's face had closed down, reconfiguring into those hard contours that had softened of late. 'Grant wants me back. *Us* back. He wants us to be a family.'

'The last thing I heard, Grant had tried to persuade you to have an abortion.' I knew as soon as the words were out of my mouth that that sharp little reality check wasn't helpful.

Nadia glared at me. 'I think everyone deserves a second chance, Mum.' She nodded in the direction of Annie. 'She's given you one.'

Annie opened her mouth to speak, but I gave a tiny shake of my head in warning.

My optimistic nature had never subscribed to the idea widely touted that if something seemed too good to be true, it probably was. But more fool me for thinking that I'd be able to right my maternal wrongs by being an exemplary grandmother to Flora.

I managed to say in a tone bordering on calm, 'Sorry,

darling, I was a bit shocked. I had no idea you were even considering returning to England. But you must, of course, give yourselves a chance to be a family.'

My first instinct was to memorise the joyful recognition in Flora's eyes when I wandered into sight. My second thought was that Nancy, Annie's mother, would be looking down on me from the heavens and squealing in triumphant elation that I might have found her daughter but I'd lost my own.

Then I mumbled something about needing to hang out the washing and hurried back into the house as fast as I could before my desperate heart allowed selfish and cruel words to do some irretrievable damage.

23

In the lead-up to Annie, Nadia and Flora leaving, I never managed to exhaust my sadness reserves. If there'd been a way to harness my sorrow and convert it to energy, I could have solved the world's resource problem there and then. Marina kept urging me to 'stop thinking about them leaving and make the most of every day they're here', which was so ridiculously simplistic, it put me in such a bad mood that even Strega panting too loudly annoyed me. The English – and Italian – language was so inadequate, lacking as it did the terminology to describe the conflicting emotions of wringing every drop of joy out of the last days with people you love while simultaneously falling apart at their impending departures.

After ten weeks, but only six when I knew Annie's real identity, I still felt more confident that I'd have an ongoing relationship with her than I did with Nadia and Flora despite the growing trust between us. As doomsday drew closer, I had the sense that Annie was making memories as much as I was.

Sleep eluded me more and more, which played right into Annie's hands as she was both a lark and an owl. We took to nipping out on the Vespa at the crack of dawn to take photos for what she called her 'Alone in Rome with Ronnie' collage – capturing all the touristy places with no one else there. I'd never been part of the selfie brigade before. Despite trying to move with the times, I'd failed to dodge the belief that photos were for birthdays and family groups at Christmas rather than providing evidence to the world that you did indeed drink wine on a Tuesday night.

Early morning was our friend. The florist in Piazza Campo de' Fiori spent ages arranging sunflowers and roses as a magnificent backdrop for us to pose in front of at the expense of setting up his stall. A fruit and veg man delivering trays of apricots and nectarines in his three-wheeler truck insisted on hoisting us up onto the back and made us promise to cut him into the royalties if the photo went '*virale*'.

We zipped about, positioning ourselves in front of the Trevi Fountain at 5.30 a.m. when we could actually appreciate its beauty.

'Throw two coins into the water,' I instructed.

'Why two?' Annie asked, flinging a couple of euros over her shoulder.

'Haven't you seen *Three Coins in a Fountain*? If you throw one, you'll come back to Rome. If you throw two, you'll fall in love with an attractive Italian...'

Annie pretended to dive in and rescue a coin. 'That's the last thing I need. No more men for me. I'd rather have a dog.'

'I'd be fully in favour of the handsome Italian if it meant you came to live out here.'

She laughed and leaned against the Vespa. 'You've already got Beth returning to hook up with Rico in the autumn. You'll be causing an exodus of middle-aged women from the UK if you're not careful.'

I gripped her hand. 'Come and visit me.' It was staggering how much I would miss the woman I'd taught myself to exist without for the best part of half a century.

'I most certainly will. But I'm holding you to the promise of coming to England too.'

And for the first time in well over forty years, the prospect enticed rather than scared me.

'Will you have a go at persuading Lyndsey to pop over here at some point? I'd love to see her.' I tried so hard to keep the pleading out of my voice.

'I will definitely be back. I'll do my best with Lyndsey.'

'Have you had any more contact with her?' I asked, with that reticence of not wanting the wrong answer to taint our last couple of weeks together.

'I've been brave. I sent her a message this morning saying that I was sorry for not understanding her point of view. That I'd realised that after people die, it seems strangely important to nail down the hard facts about them rather than letting them exist in the nebulous tangle that we allow when people are alive. That I couldn't fix anything with Mum and Dad now, but the greatest homage we could pay them was to be generous-spirited with each other.'

'Well done. Has she replied?'

Annie shook her head. 'Not yet. I've done what I can.'

It was my turn to lay my cards on the table. 'If I'm the stumbling block to you having a relationship with her, you'll have to cut me out of your life.' It was the right thing to say but I still sent up a huge wish into the universe that it wouldn't be necessary.

Annie's eyes filled. 'I hope it doesn't come to that. I keep having little bursts of excitement about introducing you to Dylan and Owen. Especially Dylan. He's adventurous and interested in people, just like you are.'

'I'd love that but you absolutely have to play the long game.' I tried to make a joke. 'I'd bet that Lyndsey will live many more years than me, so she's going to be more use to you than I am.'

It had the opposite effect. Annie burst into tears. 'I feel like

I've been looking all my life to find the person who really under-stands me again.'

We hugged, unabashed and easily. Love was such an odd emotion. We spent most of our lives taking it for granted and often only appreciated its intensity and power when it was under threat or categorically too late.

In the last week before everyone left, I spent long stints caring for Flora, reaping the benefit of Nadia wanting to have her hair cut and refresh her wardrobe. I got the impression that Nadia was determined to present herself to Grant as a woman who, despite now being a mother, had not lost her sense of self. I wrote down the litany of instructions so that I wouldn't mess up and sabotage my precious remaining time: 'Don't take Flora out after ten-thirty. Make sure the sunshade is up on the pram. Use the bottles of expressed milk starting from the left, put her over the right shoulder after a feed...'

I had a couple of days with Flora when Nadia was out for six hours at a time. I drank her in, my mind whirring with how I could be part of her life. I could visit twice, three times a year. I couldn't stay with Nadia, though. That would be a sure-fire way to fall out. Better if they came out here for the summer. Perhaps she'd be able to work from here for a month or two. Would Grant allow that? Was Nadia a wife who would be dictated to?

The coolness in our relationship over the last six years meant I didn't really know what Nadia would put up with and what she wouldn't. She'd refused to be forced into an abortion, but she hadn't stuck to her guns of disdaining any contact with a man who had tried to push her into one. My heart sank at having to stay on the right side of Grant.

Marina and I had spent entire evenings entertaining each other with his faults. 'Why does he sound as though he's making an effort to speak slowly and simplify his language for us?' Marina asked. 'He does know you were born in England?'

'I reckon he divides people into two categories: those he deems bright enough to keep up with his superior intellect and the other ninety per cent of us. I don't think he's that bothered about having an actual discussion anyway as long as he can showcase his intellect,' I said.

Every other sentence of Grant's conversation was backed up by a survey, statistics, something he'd read in *The Economist*, *The Guardian*, *New Statesman*, a trumpeting of his knowledge, rather than an exchange of ideas. And if that was how he judged people, then he was right: ninety per cent of us had no chance of even knowing whether what he'd said was accurate or just some blarney he'd pulled out of his backside. He would become apoplectic when I said I didn't watch the news any more because I found it too depressing. The last time I'd seen him, he'd accused me of being a smug grey pounder who didn't care about the world I was leaving behind for the next generation. I'd corrected him. I did care, but at my age, I'd had to choose one hill to die on and that was supporting charities that worked with domestic violence victims. 'It doesn't mean I don't care about the rest, but I don't have the energy to question every single action – I live as well as I can, within my limits.'

However, if tolerating him was the price of having a relationship with my daughter and granddaughter, I would not merely tolerate him but positively embrace him. At least, at a distance of nearly twelve hundred miles, that was my firm intention.

A couple of days before Annie, Nadia and Flora were poised to depart in a triumvirate that held my heart in their hands, I took myself off to the non-Catholic cemetery in Testaccio. I'd recommended it to Beth in her last few days in Rome as a place to find peace and now I hoped it would work the same magic for me.

I couldn't string two thoughts together while I imagined what was happening inside the apartments in my palazzo – drawers opening and closing as the contents were transferred to suitcases, the fridge being whittled down to skeleton sustenance, decisions made about whether half a bottle of shampoo merited space in the luggage. All the time, Flora's cries and smiles tucked away behind the door, gold coins pouring through my fingers like pebbles down a drain.

I parked outside the cemetery and headed through the cypress trees towards the view of the Pyramid of Cestius. I stopped to appreciate the oleander and hydrangeas, pausing in the shade of the pine trees and closing my eyes to focus on the birdsong. The singing was so vibrant, it felt as though half of the birds in Rome were in on the secret of a quiet paradise in a chaotic city where they could make themselves heard. I stood examining for a moment the towering spikes of *Acanthus mollis*, or bear's breeches as I'd known it in the UK. The glossy spires of green foliage transported me immediately to Cornwall, where the white flowers hooded with purple stood sentry-like along the coastal paths of my youth. I had a memory, as clear as though the curtains had been pulled back to reveal a spotlit stage, of Annie demanding to know why it was called bear's breeches when nothing about it looked like a pair of trousers. Life had a habit of circling back. My story had started with Annie in Cornwall and all these years later had curved to Rome, spiralling back to Britain now and taking the two other people I loved dearly with her.

I sat on a bench near Keats' grave, drawn as always to his unconventional headstone with its inscription, 'This Grave contains all that was Mortal of a young English poet'. In my early days in Rome, I'd felt an affinity with Keats that I would never have admitted to anyone for fear of sounding pretentious.

He'd gambled on a last roll of the dice, taking a boat to Italy in search of a warmer climate to cure his tuberculosis. I'd come to rejuvenate my broken and bedraggled spirit. He'd left behind the love of his life knowing that he was unlikely to see her again, though probably harbouring the hope that he would. I'd done the same with Heather and Lyndsey.

And now, unlike Keats, who'd died three months after arriving in Rome, life had delivered me a second chance. Not only had I got back the girl – now woman – whom I thought I'd lost forever, but in Flora, there was a new opportunity to love unreservedly. To build a bonfire of the mistakes I'd made with Nadia, excavate all that was good and wise from what I'd learnt, and fashion something original, true and powerful from the embers.

A middle-aged couple with matching baseball caps stood directly in front of Keats' grave, blocking my view. They read the entire inscription out loud, 'Here lies One Whose Name was writ in Water', breaking into the peace where my thoughts meandered. I registered the resentment that comes with being first at a beauty spot and regarding anyone else's presence as a trespass. The baritone of the man boomed out as he narrated bursts of Keats' Wikipedia entry. He infuriated me with his mocking tone as he read out Keats' love letter to Fanny Brawne: 'I have been astonished that Men could die Martyrs for religion – I have shudder'd at it – I shudder no more – I could be martyr'd for my Religion – Love is my religion – I could die for that – I could die for you.'

Even to my heart, that had, from necessity, grown a carapace not easily pierced, they were some of the most beautiful words ever written.

I glared at the logo on the back of the man's baggy T-shirt, the name of a pub or club or maybe a sports team, feeling an unexpected kinship with Marina's snobbiness – 'All these people who can only exist in the world by being part of a pack. So utterly unoriginal.'

Finally, his companion, who was slugging water from an oversized bottle, felt the heat of my stare and hurried him along. I had a sharp burst of satisfaction that my outward appearance of a cantankerous old woman had done the trick, even if inside I still shied away from confrontation, unable to shrug off my penchant for a smooth and harmonious world.

As the silence settled around me again, I stumbled towards the notion I'd been afraid to unpick: if everyone I loved was in England, surely I was cutting off my nose to spite my face by refusing to consider living anywhere other than Rome.

A little leap of optimism vibrated through me. I could sell off three of the apartments in the block, keep mine and Marina's and buy a place near Nadia, see Flora every day. Spend some weekends with Annie, meet her sons, perhaps even become accepted as an adopted grandmother. Maybe Lyndsey might warm to me eventually, take my story full circle. I could confront the ghosts of my past, live out my final years surrounded by the people who mattered to me. I wasn't sure how I'd break that news to Marina. Perhaps she'd come with me. Or visit for several months a year. She'd be angry, incensed at my change in circumstances impacting on hers. It was hard to imagine a daily existence devoid of her crabby belligerence.

I sat for over two hours, a stray cat occasionally purring around my legs, weighing up the eternal see-saw of life. How every decision that favoured one person necessarily sucked a bit of ballast from another. I'd expected to have to choose between Nadia and Annie. It hadn't occurred to me that I'd end up torn between Italy and England, prioritising my daughter with whom I had a precarious relationship over my best friend who was solid as a rock. After a lifetime of espousing the principle that friends were the family you chose for yourself, it had turned out that blood was indeed thicker than water. I prayed that Marina would surprise me with one last generous act of support.

As the sun peaked in the sky, I marched back to the entrance, full of the sort of energy that comes from knowing there are still many mountains to climb but having a clear idea of which direction to pick in order to reach the summit. I accelerated on my elderly Vespa in a manner that made it whine with effort. I flicked the fob on the gates, impatient to burst through them, buoyed with the enthusiasm of brandishing a plan that was both daring and obvious.

Annie and Nadia were in the garden, sitting in the shade with Flora. I'd loved seeing my daughter grow in confidence, trusting her instincts about what Flora needed. I hurried over, giddy with nerves and shaky with the bravado of confounding their expectations of what I'd find the courage to do at this stage of my life.

I stroked Flora's cheek with my finger. 'Hello, my darling princess,' I said, and was rewarded with a gummy smile.

Nadia frowned. 'Don't call her that.'

'What?'

'Princess. She's not to grow up thinking that she's some helpless damsel sitting in a tower, waiting to be rescued by a man, or that the only way she can achieve in life is to be born into the right family.'

'Sorry.' It wouldn't matter how hard I tried, I'd never pick the right words to meet Nadia's exacting standards. 'It's just a term of endearment, I don't think like that. Of course she's going to be an independent and clever little thing who won't need any rescuing,' I said, tickling Flora's toes. Nadia knew that.

'As Heschel said, "Words create worlds".' Her tone had softened, but the certainty that her view was the one that counted still reverberated loud and clear.

I glanced at Annie to see if she knew who Heschel was. If I

had to be an ignoramus, it was nice to have company. She rescued me. 'Who was he?'

Grant's puzzled expression in the presence of anyone who wasn't au fait with every philosopher/poet/historian of the last four centuries was obviously contagious. Nadia tucked her chin in, her mouth dropping open, as though she was unable to believe our lack of culture. 'A rabbi, a Jewish theologian and philosopher.'

'Wise words,' I said, wondering if Nadia and Grant had a calendar with three hundred and sixty-five inspirational quotes that they memorised on a daily basis.

I tried to ignore my glimpse into a future where Nadia and Grant would be monitoring every word, every action, hypervigilant about my influence in case I allowed Flora to dress up as a fairy. By sheer dint of will, I smothered the creeping suspicion that rather than a win-win situation of free childcare in exchange for glorious and liberated hours with Flora in a chaos of crayons and crafts, Nadia would have a plan. A checklist of fresh air, tambourine practice, chickpea puree, drawing classes, as well as many other horrors for the improvement and instruction of toddlers that I didn't have the imagination to conjure up.

Annie brought light to the conversation. 'You were out and about early. Where have you been?'

I explained how the non-Catholic cemetery was my go-to place when I wanted to think things through. 'I like sitting by Keats' grave. It sounds silly, but I feel a bit of a connection with him because he left England for Rome and never went back.'

Nadia frowned. 'That's because he died after three months. It's not quite the same, Mum. And, anyway, you have been back.'

It was a character trait Nadia had, always feeling the need to correct my version of a story, to have an opinion on how I should tell or interpret it.

I didn't reply and faced Annie, who was just the opposite,

smiling in that way she had, demonstrating an interest in your ideas, confidence in your ability. 'And did you have any light-bulb moments?'

I took a breath, waiting for the words 'I was wondering about selling up here and buying somewhere in England' to rush out, an exciting concept that would make Annie and Nadia leap up, piling in with suggestions, with help, with eagerness. I faltered. My plan to move to England, my bold and brilliant strategy for us all to spend more time together, the idea that had been sparkling with possibility and promise seemed a little duller, tarnished even. Less than an hour had elapsed and my vision of the future was already withering around the edges.

I gave Flora's big toe a last little tweak. 'I thought about how much I've loved having you all here. How much I'll miss you. But also how glad I am that Villa Alba has worked its magic and that you're both going back to England in a better place than you were when you arrived.' My heart hammered as I grappled with how to present my idea of joining them over there.

'Will you come and visit me? Maybe in the autumn? Meet the kids?' Annie checked herself. 'My adult sons.'

She had such an easy way about her, allowing me to receive an invitation without weighing up the obligation she felt to host versus the genuine desire for my company. Perhaps that was only possible among people who weren't related, whom blood ties didn't bind in a tug of war between duty and powerful, primeval love.

'I'd love that. And, of course, you're welcome here any time, all of you.'

Except I might not be here, I might be living in a little flat around the corner from Nadia. Although, as I didn't seem to be able to construct a single sentence alluding to that possibility, the odds of it happening were currently appearing rather remote.

Annie turned to Nadia. 'You're only an hour away from me

across London. If you want a break or a night out on the town with Grant, I'll happily – *happily* – look after Flora for you.'

Nadia's face broke into a big grin. 'Be careful what you offer. I might take you up on that, thank you.'

I embraced the delight that people I loved were building a relationship whilst battling a sense of exclusion that they'd be doing things together that I longed to join in with.

'I'll really miss being in Rome,' Nadia said, smoothing her hair back behind her ears.

We all sat in silence as we contemplated the events of this summer. I longed to say something meaningful, stateswomanly, memorable to sum up the intensity of this time. To stun them with the knowledge that I valued them so highly I was planning to move back to England after all these years. To make sure they knew that meeting my granddaughter, reconnecting with Nadia and finding Annie again were the highlights of this decade, if not the rest of my life. It was astonishing how difficult it was to risk saying it out loud, fearful that my heart might not endure a dismissive response from Nadia.

However, I found myself hoist by my own petard of assuming the worst of my daughter, who burrowed her face into Flora's neck as she said, 'I'm so grateful to you, Mum, thank you. I was a bit naïve about what having a baby would be like.'

'Everyone is, darling. We all think that the horror stories can't possibly be true, that it will be better for us. Otherwise why would any of us disrupt our lives with a baby? But what you can't explain, simply can't put into words, is the intense joy they bring that – at some point – makes up for the rest.'

'Did you feel like that with me?' Nadia asked.

'It's hard to remember now, though I'm sure I did. The one thing I can guarantee, a hundred per cent, is that I have never ever wished I hadn't had you.' I had to stop bracing myself, accept that we could have genuine and kind exchanges, that we could train ourselves out of this need to protect ourselves from each other.

Out of the corner of my eye, I saw Annie slip away and I loved her more than ever.

In a rare burst of vulnerability, Nadia said, 'I'm not sure that Grant and I will make it.'

'But you're giving it a go. That's all you can do. Give it the very best shot you can. Better to die trying than die wondering.' My turn to sound like the inspirational quote calendar.

Now was my moment. The moment I should tell her that I'd be right by her side – literally and geographically – to help her through. Still the words stuck in my throat.

Nadia laid Flora in her pram, covering her with a sheet, placing her hands gently over the top. One of many tiny gestures that would knit together to form a cradle of care. As I watched my daughter, this child I'd grown, nourished and nurtured, often imperfectly, sometimes irritably, occasionally resentfully, I recognised that instead of forcing myself into her life, I had to choose to let her go. To accept that my reward would come from seeing her flourish, not from keeping her close by. My role now was to allow her room to find happiness, her rhythm, without trying to shape her decisions with my own preferences. I would always struggle to understand what she saw in Grant, would probably always find him a bombastic bore. But sniping from the sidelines wouldn't help, especially if Flora became a pawn in a power struggle I should never have entered into. Could never enter into, in fact.

With a rush of sadness mingled with conviction, I felt the relief of certainty: I had to release her onto her own path through motherhood. It had been madness to consider uprooting myself now. Rome was my home. In England, I would become a burden, clingy and needy. I had no connection to Britain now outside of Nadia and Annie. Time with Flora would become a prop, a vital source of entertainment rather than a carefree pleasure. Of course, there was a part of me that yearned for the luxury of living within a popping-in radius, of experiencing many ordinary minutes rather than infrequent red-letter days. But I'd lived my life, made my choices – good and bad – and Nadia needed to do the same.

I swallowed. 'If it doesn't work out, there will always be a home for you here. Think of Marina and me as a safety net – you'll probably never need us, but we'll be ready to catch you.'

'I'll miss you. We both will.' She squeezed my hand. 'Will you come for Christmas?'

They were words I'd never thought Nadia would ever utter, a simple invitation taken for granted by so many mothers but never by me. I felt a prickle at the back of my eyes considering how much Flora would have changed by then, how much I'd enjoy witnessing her delight at the fairy lights. 'I'd love to, of course. But you and Grant and Flora are going to need a bit of time to settle. To adjust from being a couple, to a couple with a child, and finally to a family. See how you feel later in the year.'

'I really want Flora to have a relationship with you, Mum.'

I breathed through the sob that was threatening to come wailing out of my chest. 'Well, I want that too, so I'm sure we can make it happen. You two are the most important people in my world.'

'What about Annie?'

'She's important too.' I resisted the urge to diminish Annie in order to curry favour with Nadia.

Nadia put her little finger into Flora's fist. 'Do you wish she was your real daughter instead of me?'

'No, of course not!' I paused for a moment, to inspect the truth of that. 'No. No, I don't.'

I didn't feel I could say my next words sitting beside Nadia. They were words that needed space, room to look away as I delivered them.

I stood up and started fiddling about, picking at the spent

heads of my lavender. 'I loved Annie, her sister too, when they were little. It broke something in me when I was banned from seeing them. I was frightened of loving that freely again. So with your dad, with you, I kept holding back; I was afraid to risk that level of hurt. And I'm sorry, because I should have been braver. I wish I'd made loss a springboard into making the most of everything, of living right in the moment, of loving as much as I possibly could, instead of fearing what might happen in the future. I've wasted so much time being half in and half out. But I want you to know, Nadia, that for the rest of my days, however long I've got, I will do my best to be the mother you should have had in the first place.'

I turned my head to look at Nadia. She bit her lip. 'Flora is already teaching me that it's not as easy as it looks.' She walked towards me and held out her arms.

I leaned against her, breathing her in, already attempting to commit her scent to memory. 'Let's try really hard to believe the best of each other.'

24

Eventually, like an operation I'd been dreading but knew I'd have to undergo before I could march along the road to recovery, the final afternoon arrived. I waved off the little tribe that had brought life and light to Villa Alba. The meaningful words I'd intended to impart as the closing curtain call were lost in a last-minute nappy incident. The ensuing clean-up operation negated the possibility of a long drawn-out goodbye. I had to forgo the heart-wounding drama I usually brought to these scenes. I'd be all business-like, with a brisk hug intended to side-step the looming swell of emotion. Immediately afterwards, I'd have a sense of not completing the requirements of a proper farewell, which would prompt a demand for a second and final hug. Nadia would acquiesce with the impatience of someone who delivered embraces on a strictly rationed basis. I'd end up hanging on a fraction too long, veering between the anticipation of living life to my own drumbeat versus the surge of loss that enveloped me. Inevitably, I was always conscious of a dissatisfaction that our time together had never quite lived up to its potential. That amongst the companionable days, there'd been a surplus of petty grievances and snappy exchanges. Intermingled into this desperate clutch was a catastrophising dart of fear that I might never see her again, that the finger of fate would choose today to strike. I lived in dread that my last memory of Nadia would be a lecture about how much electricity I was wasting by not packing the empty spaces in my freezer with newspaper.

Today, in the flurry of fishing a clean sleepsuit out of Nadia's case, there was no time for anything but a rapid kiss to mark the first goodbye with my granddaughter. A quick but warm embrace from Annie. 'Thank you. For everything. For opening your house to me, as well as your heart.' By way of a response, I nodded and pressed the heels of my hands into my eye sockets. She squeezed my arm. 'You haven't seen the last of me,' she said.

'Good.' Such a small word to be in charge of such a huge amount of hope.

Next came a tight and heartfelt but brief hug from Nadia, who was frantically double-checking her documents, zipping and unzipping pockets and bearing scant resemblance to the woman who used to regard international travel as no more stressful than a tram to Trastevere.

'Bye, Mum. Bye, Marina. Thanks for everything. Love you.'

I waved through the taxi window at Flora, who gazed back blankly, a tiny tyrant with an indifferent heart. I shouted, 'Love you all, travel safely,' my words fading into the hot August air.

The courtyard gates closed behind them and I stood for a moment, allowing the leaving to settle and the living without them to begin.

Marina tapped her stick on the ground. 'I feel like I've lived twelve years in those twelve weeks.' She set off towards the steps. 'Come on, shall we choose another victim? Perhaps the next one will reveal that you're an exiled queen and there's an abandoned palace awaiting your return in a far-flung municipality.'

I swiped at the tears running down my cheeks. 'I can assure

you there's no blue blood to report,' I said. 'I think I need a break from the bereaved and the birthing.'

'Negroni sbagliato?'

I nodded.

We sat on Marina's roof terrace, as the afternoon drifted into the evening, sipping our drinks and leafing through her stack of *Oggi* magazines, commenting on the celebrity gossip and allowing the intensity of the last few weeks to subside. Family and rediscovered nearly family were wonderful, but frivolity was a fantastic counterbalance to allow the emotional wells to replenish. Even Strega seemed delighted to have my full attention, poking me with her nose every time I stopped stroking her.

As I scanned the night sky for shooting stars, quietly hoping for a sign from the universe that all was as it should be, Marina appeared with a platter of salami and her tomato bruschetta that packed a garlicky punch.

'*Tutto bene*? Are you sad?'

'A bit hollow, but it's almost like letting a baby bird you've nursed back to health go free. It's hard to be really sad because they're doing exactly what they should be.'

Marina arched an eyebrow. 'And you – are you doing what you should be? You're not about to run out on me and move back to England to spend more time with them all, are you?'

'I did consider it.' I couldn't quite meet Marina's stare.

'That's not going to happen.' Then Marina stopped as though it had only now occurred to her that we didn't live in a dictatorship. 'Would you really leave Rome? And me?' she asked, waving her hands about theatrically, as though she was everyone's raison d'être, not just mine.

'I'm not going to say never, because never is a long time.'

'You're not getting rid of me that easily.'

But before we could get into a futile discussion about an improbable future, my phone beeped and a WhatsApp message came through. A photo of Annie and Lyndsey with the caption: *Guess who met me at the airport???!*

I thrust it under Marina's nose. 'Look at this! The healing power of Villa Alba.'

She lifted her glass. 'To us, to them, to this city and its seven glorious hills.' She took a sip of her drink. 'To always knowing what's best for everyone else.'

A LETTER FROM KERRY

Dear Reader,

I want to say a huge thank you for choosing to read *Secrets at the Rome Apartment*. If you did enjoy it, and want to keep up to date with all my latest releases, just sign up at the following link. Your email address will never be shared and you can unsubscribe at any time.

www.bookouture.com/kerry-fisher

I lived in Florence and Tuscany for five years in my twenties, working as a grape picker, a holiday rep, a guidebook researcher and a personal assistant to the director of an art school. Most of the ex-pat friends I made while I was living there have eventually found their way back to their home countries, but we have remained united, thirty years on, by our love for Italy (and each other!). We all agree that there is something magical about that country and all of us have returned regularly.

In 2022, my husband and I finally had the time and opportunity to spend a month in Rome. I hadn't planned for our time there to be a research trip, viewing it instead as a chance to live in the city and experience it in a different way from my usual approach to sightseeing (which is to get up at the crack of dawn and race about trying to see everything in four days!). I had dipped a toe in the water writing scenes against an Italian backdrop before – the country has a cameo role in *After the Lie*, *The Silent Wife* and *The Woman I Was Before* – but I've never set an entire book there.

However, as soon as I arrived in Rome, the creative possibilities started jostling for attention – it's hard to ignore the inspiration offered up by all those eye-catching doorways and the enticing courtyards beyond, the little curiosities around every corner. I spent an awful lot of time people watching, and from there, the little acorn of an idea grew about how everyone in a family has a different narrative about their upbringing. I'm also fascinated by how people who love each other can easily fall out because of their deep conviction that there is only one right way to live, with both parties desperate to convert the other person to their superior way of thinking.

It was an absolute privilege to experience a month away from 'normal life' – the luxury of time to dream, to wander and wonder without the daily urgency to get things done. Rome has an energy all of its own – I walked miles and miles every day and could have stayed for much longer without tiring of it. No matter how often I passed through the same streets, there was always something new to see – the gesticulating inherent in any conversation, a stained-glass window catching the sun, olive oil sold from the bonnet of a car, the Swiss Guards emerging in their colourful uniforms from an alleyway, an impromptu dance display near the Colosseum, the stylish hats and gloves...

I found my whole time there so invigorating. Consequently, it wasn't a huge leap to come up with a scenario about how a woman with a past she'd like to leave behind might find comfort in starting again in such a beautiful city. *Secrets at the Rome Apartment* was the result and I hope you loved it. If you did, I would be very grateful if you could write a review. I'd love to know what you think, and it makes a real difference in helping new readers to discover one of my books for the first time.

I love hearing from my readers – you can get in touch on my

Facebook page, through Twitter, or my website. Your messages never fail to brighten my day.

Thank you so much for reading,

Kerry Fisher

www.kerryfisherauthor.com

 facebook.com/kerryfisherauthor
twitter.com/KerryFSwayne

ACKNOWLEDGEMENTS

'Thank you' seems a rather underwhelming expression for the gratitude I feel for the support of my editor, Jenny Geras. Her vision always plays a significant role in transforming my scrappy half-baked ideas into fully formed stories – a feat she pulls off with grace and patience, and no more so than with this second book in my Rome series.

Huge thanks to the Bookouture production team working their magic to make the finished product the best it can possibly be – plus the wonderful publicity team – Kim, Noelle, Sarah and Jess – who do a great job of connecting our books with the right readership.

Thank you to the brilliant Clare Wallace, my agent – I've been so lucky to have you championing my books over the last ten years. Also to the rights team at Darley Anderson who've worked so hard to make sure my novels have reached readers everywhere from Estonia to Brazil.

Thank you to birth doula Leila Gardiner for talking me through childbirth and home births – all mistakes are mine (though I've done it twice and really felt I should be a bit more knowledgeable than I turned out to be!). Also to Serena Boscarato for checking my Italian.

I couldn't finish my acknowledgements without saying a massive thank you to all my readers – you are the best cheer-leaders – I love the conversations and interactions I have with you on my author Facebook page. Your enthusiasm for my books really gives me a lift when the going gets tough.

And finally, my family, especially Steve, for responding to my texts of the teapot emoji with speed and good humour. I'm lucky to have you all.

Made in the USA
Monee, IL
08 October 2023

44164574R00125